Peter Smart's Confessions

PAUL BAILEY'S first novel, *At the Jerusalem* (1967), won three prizes, including the Somerset Maugham Award. This was followed by *Trespasses* (1970) and *A Distant Likeness* (1973). In 1974 he received the E. M. Forster Award from the American Academy of Arts and Letters, and in 1977 the George Orwell Memorial Prize. *Peter Smart's Confessions* (1977) was shortlisted for the Booker Prize. *Old Soldiers* appeared in 1980, and *Gabriel's Lament* (also shortlisted for the Booker Prize) in 1986. His other books include the memoir *An Immaculate Mistake* (1990), *Sugar Cane* (1993) and his latest novel, *Kitty & Virgil* (1998). He edited *The Oxford Book of London*, published in 1995.

Peter Smart's Confessions

Paul Bailey

FOURTH ESTATE • *London*

This paperback edition published in 2000 by
Fourth Estate Limited
6 Salem Road
London W2 4BU
www.4thestate.co.uk

1 3 5 7 9 10 8 6 4 2

A catalogue record for this book is available from the British Library

ISBN 978-0-00-729277-6

Printed in Great Britain by Cox & Wyman Ltd, Reading

Contents

For Anna Pugh

Paradise Gained

He had succeeded at last. Never again would he suffer humiliation and defeat. He was with the majority now.

He saw a buxom angel approaching. He would accept her apologies for Saint Peter's absence humbly and gratefully: 'How kind of him to send you.' He reckoned she must be Muriel, whom God had appointed to represent the month of June. The skilful manner in which she jumped over each dangerous stretch of blue proved her to be one well acquainted with the peculiar hazards of celestial life.

Muriel passed without a word. Her raiment, he noticed, had lost its sheen. It had the washed-out look of hospital clothes.

He waited. Other angels came and went. They were all as drably dressed as Muriel, and like her they ignored him. Did the fools imagine that he would be upset by their indifference? He smiled at the notion. He was beyond such mundane hurts: he was extinct, and he felt radiant.

In this blissful condition, he looked about him. There was nothing here to enchant the eye or quicken the heart. Heaven, he realized, must have its suburbs too. God's civil servants had to function somewhere. Wingless, deprived of harps and lyres, the far from serene creatures who hurried by were obviously preoccupied with affairs of state. Cabbalists in the fourteenth century had worked out that there were 301,655,722 attendant spirits – it stood to reason, then, that they had to be a variegated lot. 'It takes all sorts,' he heard himself say. He couldn't remember ever mouthing such a commonplace on earth.

Moving more cautiously than Muriel, he set off in what he hoped was the direction of the Heavenly City. Trumpets, perhaps, would greet his arrival. Clothed in white samite, and with star-encircled heads, the angels there would be entirely glorious.

Anxious now to join that harmonious congregation, he hurried on. Death had given him a new vitality: Achilles, in peak condition, could not have run faster. His feet seemed to be thinking for him. They were already as deft as Muriel's, for the stretches of blue were no longer a challenge. Whenever they told him to leap, his body happily followed. Each cloud was attained with absolute confidence.

Several years later, he began to be fatigued. Cramp brought him to a stop. He placed his hands on his knees and took deep breaths. It was some time before the bracing air filled his lungs and he was able to stand upright. The view hadn't changed. He was no nearer his goal.

He would soon die of boredom in this place. His yawn turned into a laugh and then the laugh became something like a shriek of terror as the appalling irony hit him. He couldn't die of anything any more. There were no pills here to dispatch him. There was nowhere else to go. It seemed that he had failed again.

He would get to God's capital if it was the last thing he did. The days of doubt were over. He would start off as soon as he felt refreshed. His limbs were itching for movement, and his feet were tingling.

Suddenly—as if someone had pulled a switch—the music of the spheres could be heard. He listened. It sounded nothing like Mozart. It sounded horrible. It sounded, this untidy counterpoint, like one of the many insignificant works of Siegfried Günter, the only tone-deaf son of Johann Sebastian Bach. He tried to put his hands to his ears, but his arms were paralysed.

While he was doing his best not to listen, his mother—improbably angelic—wafted by. He had his chance now; now he could ask her that question he had never had the courage to put to her down below: 'Mother, did you poison Father?' He raced after her. He blocked her path. She smiled at him with new teeth. He opened his mouth, but instead of words the sound of a violin came out. His mother blew him a kiss, rose in the air until she was above his head, and then flew away.

The violin inside him refused to stop. A cherub, not unlike the mischievous imp to the bottom right of Raphael's Sistine Madonna, shot up from the cloud he was standing on, pointed a chubby finger at him, let out a surprisingly deep laugh, and disappeared.

Something solid and disgusting replaced the music in his throat. It was an earthly substance – phlegm, or bile. It threatened to choke him. A ministering angel parted his lips. He was continually, violently sick.

'Into the bowl. That's where we want it.'
I retched.
'One more try. There's only a little left.'
The after-life – I remember thinking – has its discomforts, too.
'Sit up now, Mr Smart.'
'Are you Muriel?'
'My name's Eunice. We don't have anyone called Muriel here.'
'I saw her a few minutes ago –
'You did, did you?'
'She's an angel.'
'With wings?'
'No. She doesn't have any.'
'Poor girl. Perhaps the almoner's looking after them. Don't worry. I'll see she gets them back.'
'Who are you?'
'If you put your head up, you'll find out.'
I saw a black woman. She was dressed as a nurse. She was smiling at me.
'Intensive care,' she said. Then, laughing like the cherub, she repeated the words.
I was in a hospital ward. Blood was dripping slowly into the arm of a young girl. In the next bed, an old man lay moaning.
'Intensive care!'
'Oh, no.'
'Oh, yes.'
'Have I failed again?'

'That's what it looks like. Man, you don't mean to say you took those tablets before? You sure are a crazy one. If I see too much of you, I'll be needing intensive care as well.'

I pinched myself, to check. This was real. I was no longer radiant.

'How's Lazarus?' The doctor's grey eyes settled on me briefly. 'Is he out of the cave, Miss McGregor?'

'He's alive.'

'Give him some stewed tea and send him home.'

I tried, haltingly, to apologize.

'You're an idiot,' the doctor broke in. 'A loon—that's what you are. I don't know why I'm expected to keep patience with you and your kind, but I am. Why didn't you do it properly?'

'I thought I had.'

'You should have thought more clearly. Take a look along the ward, my friend. There are people dying here. There are people here in scarcely bearable pain. You have wasted my time.'

'I thought I'd succeeded for once.'

'Your thoughts need thinking about, Mr Smart. That's my diagnosis. What did you give your dog—Nembutal?'

'Dog?'

'Dog.'

'You must mean Fu Manchu.'

'I don't know who I mean.'

'He's a Pekingese. He's a monster. He's my wife's.'

'You swallowed his tranquillizers when you were drunk.'

'How ridiculous.'

'Aren't you? It's a pity you don't appeal to my sense of humour. Drink less the next time. You might find your hands grasping the right bottle.'

Ether and cabbage: first one smell, then the other, then the two together. My blood pulsed at a quicker rate as I recalled the morning of Stephen's birth—Nancy's long agony; the moment when his head appeared. As I sniffed, the tiny body emerged again, vividly red in the dark corridor.

The nurse said she was pleased to see me smiling. Although she'd enjoyed my company, I was to take her advice and not come a second time to the intensive care unit: Dr Thornton might polish me off, and that would upset her.

Shame prevented me from telling her about the shame I knew she was wholly aware of.

'He was just moody. He has those days.'

'He was right to be angry with me.'

'His ears go up and down when he's cross. I was biting my lip while he was shouting at you.'

She was silent until we reached the entrance hall.

'Don't you do as he says. You make sure you drink yourself silly.'

She shook both my hands. We went out on to the steps and said goodbye.

When I was near the gates, I heard her call my name. I turned. She was making her arms flap like wings.

'Is that how Muriel does it? When she has them?'

'I should think so.'

She slapped her cheeks gently, and laughed. I waved.

I rested the limbs I had not succeeded in disposing of on one of London's forlorn strips of grass. I opened an evening paper someone had left near by and read of common horrors – famine in India; a murder in Glasgow; a baby abandoned in a public lavatory; things like that.

I hummed loudly to drown the doctor's insults. What a strange word he'd used: 'loon'. I started to sing. And then the reference to Lazarus; his asking the nurse if I was out of the cave ... He was (clearly) an oblique creature, for all his directness.

A boy strolled past, eating roast chicken from a paper box. My recently emptied stomach growled a message to my reluctantly functioning brain. A second, louder growl brought in its wake the urge to shed tears compounded of shame and joy. I stood up, hoping that my feet would get me to my flat as speedily as they had not got me to God's headquarters. I needed to weep in private over a plate of nourishing food.

I sat for over an hour, staring at nothing in particular, before I remembered that I was hungry. I went to the kitchen and made myself an omelette with three eggs, a Jersey potato, a spring onion, a tomato, and the green tip of a cucumber that was otherwise brown. As I was eating it, standing up, I saw a note propped against the almost empty bottle of whisky I had been drinking from two nights before:

My Dear Sir. If you are still alive and arnt dead as a result then you will read this when you come home. I hope I found you in the Knick of time. Touch wood and fingers crossed. I gave you the Kiss of Life wich I enjoyed I must say. After they took you off in the ambulence (All the nosey cows in the street were out to have a look) after they took you I gave the flat a good going over for when you come home. If you dont see your face in the furniture my name is not Doris Hedley. By the way I have taken Dog. I coudnt leave him to pine and fret. My Mum says that pets are only little Humans. You can have him back to give him back to Mrs Smart when you come home. He is a ugly little sod—Pardon My French. What is his name. I shall call him Chairman Mow. He will be compeny for my Mum while I am working she is fond of animals we once had a cat. She is not her lively old self at all. She had the last of her teeth out on tuesday and a new gas cooker put in. You shoud have seen the mess but thats British Workmen. Well Sir its a lovely day if you like Heat wich I dont. Roll on September thats what I say. Well Sir that is all the news from Deptford way for this week. All being well and the worst not coming to you as a result I shall see you all cheerfull when I turn up like the Bad Penny on Friday next. I have arsked Hospital to keep me informed about your State of Health.

> Wellcome Home.
> Yours faithfully.
> DORIS HEDLEY (MISS).

I drank a toast to Doris with the last of the whisky.

At dawn I made one of my rare decisions. I would emulate my benefactor, F. Leonard Cottie, and 'venture into the field of autobiography'. There was a chance that I might make some sense, if only intermittently, of those thoughts the doctor had advised me to think about.

I began my confessions by describing how I had made a trip to Heaven, unconvincingly disguised as a contented man.

God, whom I have yet to meet, knows where and how they will end.

Childhood Pleasures

My mother sometimes called me Peter when we had company, but since we rarely had company she hardly ever called me Peter. 'You' was my name. 'You' distinguished me from the rest of humanity. Her 'You!' was a summons I had to obey.

Because of her phenomenal vocal range, she was able to use the word with an operatic dexterity. Her bass snarls frightened me more than her coloratura shrieks. Her teeth seemed to draw blood from the deep, disyllabic 'You' she employed on those occasions when my stupidity—or intelligence—particularly exasperated her. It came out slowly, dripping.

I was 'You' from an early age. I was probably 'You' while I was in my pram, but—mercifully—I can't set that down as a fact. My first memory is of a day in autumn: Mother has taken me to a park, and I'm running loose. There are piles of leaves everywhere. Whenever I come to a new pile, I stir the leaves up with my hands and feet. I jump on them and they crackle. Then I come to the biggest pile of all, and I run so far into it that the leaves completely cover me. I can taste and smell them. They aren't dry or crisp. They are sticking to my hair, my skin, my clothes. I am happy in this darkness, sticky though it is.

'The bogy-man's in there,' says Mother. 'He won't let you out if he gets hold of you.'

I thrash about now, terrified that I shall be eaten. His long black fingers are moving towards me. He will break me up bit by bit and when his tummy's full, he'll throw my bones to his dogs. That's his way with little boys.

When I open my eyes, I'm in the park once more. My mother says 'You' and removes a leaf from my nose. She takes another from my neck, saying 'You' as she throws it to the ground. She plucks several more from my pullover, and she is almost shouting: 'You!' She shakes my trousers and snarls. She's whispering by the time she reaches my socks and shoes: 'Oh–you. Oh–you.'

Her reserves of contempt–it grieves me to write–were limitless. Like everyone else in the world, 'You' could do nothing to please her. I tried many times, but 'You' always failed. I recall the Christmas after my father's death: I've come home (if that's the right word for F. Leonard Cottie's basement) with my school report in hand. I give it to her. To my astonishment, she sniffs it, and then throws it on the kitchen table.

'Aren't you going to read it?'

'You.'

'Please read it, Mother.'

'It'll keep. There'll be time enough tomorrow or the next day.'

'Please. See what it says about me.'

'It's about you, is it? Just fancy, I thought it had to do with the cat. Oh, fetch my specs, You.'

Aware of my excited state, she sits down very slowly. She then spends several minutes cleaning her already clean glasses. She opens the report with great deliberation and smooths it out on the oilcloth. I watch her closely as she begins to read.

Mother does not read *through* her glasses, but *over* them.

'Hm,' she says.

'What's that, Mother?'

'History!'

'But I was top of the class.'

'History's over. History's done. History's what's been. History won't get you far in the here and now.'

'I might write a book one day, Mother. A book of history.'

'I can see that paying for the Sunday joint.' Her body shakes briefly with soundless laughter. It stiffens again as she reads on. 'Hm.'

'What's that, Mother?'

'Top of the class in French, too.'

'Yes.'

15

'Inky pinky parleeing won't get you anywhere.'

'I could become a – a diplomat. Or a translator. Or a –'

'You. Your ideas. Where they come from, I don't know. Not from me, your mother, that's the truth. My eye-strain will be coming on, I can see, if I have to cope with more of this. A schoolmaster who writes like a spider is a disgrace. Firm of hand, firm of mind, I was taught. You remember that, You.'

'Yes, Mother.'

'Top in English as well, eh? Little Mr Clever Dick, aren't you? Well, at least it's a language people speak.'

'People speak French, Mother.'

'Only foreigners. Not real people. As far as you can trust a man whose writing slopes, he seems to think quite high of you, this master does. But then, he doesn't know the side of you that I do. Only "Good" for music. That's a relief. You won't be going mad and playing the piano with long hair in a hurry.'

'No.'

'I should hope not.'

She stabs the report with a finger. She nods vigorously many times. She stabs it again as she says, 'I thought so. I thought as much. I thought so.'

I ask her to tell me what it is she's thought.

'A fat lot of good that Hallelujah Chorus for your history, your English and your parlee-vous is if you can't do your sums!'

She slings the report away from her. It falls into a bowl of cooling fat.

I feel the need to retrieve it, but the feeling goes. Let it sink, let it drown.

I don't tell Mother that I want to die.

'Those are all things for *after* work, not for work proper. Work proper's being able to add up and to take away.'

'I can't be good at everything.'

'You could try being good at the one thing that matters. You're growing up just like your father.'

'Dad could add and subtract. How could he have worked as a clerk if he didn't know – ?'

She smiles at her fool of a son.

'Oh yes, he knew all about it. There wasn't a thing he didn't know about other people's money. That was your father's trouble – knowing how to make it for others. But did he ever make enough for himself and family? No, he did not!'

Her voice has risen to a shriek. She takes off her glasses, polishes them, and returns them to their case, which she snaps shut with a chill finality. The noise is more eloquent to me than her words.

'You, go and change into your house clothes. And take that halo from off your head at the same time. When you're as clever as Dr Cottie upstairs, that will be the day for resting on your laurels. You hear me?'

'Yes, Mother.'

'I should hope so.'

My laurels were already wilting from Mother's blight as I went to my room. I lay on my bed and longed for a fatal illness to seize my body. However much I willed it (I actually prayed to the God whose existence I was beginning to have doubts about) tuberculosis refused to put in an appearance that evening.

Years before, at my first school, I'd had a friend called Tommy. He was an ugly boy: his face and neck were purple with spots, and he wore a brace over his teeth. He smelt of the white mice his parents bred. His life had come to an end in a strange way.

He was walking home one November afternoon when a storm broke. He ran for the nearest shelter. When the rain subsided, he left Mr Gilbert's doorway and went into the street. As he did so, two slates fell off the roof and struck him on the head.

The Sunday after Tommy's death, I got up early and left the house without disturbing my parents. The sky, I saw to my dismay, was cloudless. As I turned the corner, the wind nearly knocked me over and my hopes rose. I walked the half mile or so to Mr Gilbert's house without seeing anyone. The old piano-tuner was in hospital, so I placed myself where I imagined Tommy had stood the Tuesday before, and had no fear of Mr Gilbert rushing out and ordering me to move away. Soon I would be in a box—a bit bigger than Tommy's—with flowers on top.

Stiff-backed as a soldier, and anxious not to move even an inch from my chosen spot in case the slates should miss me, I waited. I nodded when Mrs Cain, who was known as Pussy because she kept a cats'-meat stall under the railway arches, told me that Mr Gilbert was gasping his last in the Bethel. 'Looks as though the wind's blown itself off over the river,' she said as she went by. Then Mrs Notarianni, whose ices Mother forbade me to eat because of the foreign milk they were made from, passed with her six daughters, all in black. They smiled at me. But when they returned from church an hour later they gave me odd looks and said words in their language that made them laugh.

Twelve struck, and the sound brought roast beef and Yorkshire pudding to my mind. I stepped forward carefully: perhaps Tommy hadn't stood where I'd been standing, after all. I took another step. I swivelled my head round and stared up at the roof. The slates looked very secure and very still. I closed my eyes and saw meat and gravy and an enormous baked potato where the box and flowers had been.

'Come on, son,' I heard my father say. I opened my eyes. He was grinning at me. 'Trouble. Your mother.' He made his face go very cross for a second. 'It'll pass,' he said, and his smile came back.

'You, what were you up to outside Mr Gilbert's?' Mother asked as soon as we were in the hall.

I said something about going where Tommy was, in a box like his, only bigger.

'Thoughts like that will make you go cuckoo, they will. You be sensible and normal, You. You just behave. The disgrace of it, having that woman coming here.'

'Which woman?'

'That common old sow from the arches, that's who. Standing in my hall smelling of horses' insides and telling me that my son was acting daft in front of the piano-tuner's—that's who it was, You.'

I had to wait till supper-time for roast beef. Before I was

allowed to eat it, I had to promise that I would be respectable in future and not do things that would bring the cats'-meat woman into a decent place where she wasn't wanted.

While I was committing that happy memory to paper, one of the legs of my writing table suddenly snapped in half. Nancy had warned me of its imminent collapse from woodworm on her last visit—the day she delivered Fu Manchu into my unwilling hands.

I was not at all inconvenienced by this mishap. The man who possesses a copy of F. Leonard Cottie's *With Stethoscope and Scalpel*—the book that stopped a thousand doors—is unlikely to be disconcerted by so trifling an accident. I own thirteen copies of that masterwork.

With the doctor's meditations to support it, the table is steadier than ever.

My father was a man of few words, some of them consecutive. I rarely heard them, they were pitched so low. He spoke to himself at every meal, and it was not until about a year before his death that I actually began to hear what he was saying between munches. 'Boiled to buggery' came out ringingly one night, but only because Mother's upset stomach, from which she was suffering loudly in another room, ensured his safety.

If long sentences ever formed in his brain, they met with some fracturing impediment en route to his lips. His thoughts escaped in code.

We are strolling home, my father and I, on a summer evening. The war is over and London is safe to walk in. We have seen Mother on to a train at King's Cross. She will be away for a week.

'Where's Mother gone?'
'North.'
'Why, Dad?'
'Duty.'
'What's that?'

19

'Doing her duty. Conscience.'

I am mystified. Much later I ask, 'Why?' and am happy not to receive Mother's usual answer to that question: 'That's the twenty-fifth letter of the alphabet.' He says instead, 'Why what?'

'Why does she do her duty?'

'Has to. On her mind. Worries her.'

'What does?'

'Conscience.'

'Con-science?'

'Conscience. Not often. Sometimes.'

'What's conscience?'

He thinks. I wait: the mystery of Mother's yearly trip to 'where the heathens live' will soon be solved. It's because of her conscience – whatever that is.

'When your mind. The worry. You're upset. Have to do better. By others. Her mother. In her case.'

'Mother's mother?'

'That's her. Mrs Dixon.'

'Mrs Dixon?'

'That's her. Your mother – Dixon before Smart.'

So I have two grandmothers.

'Mother's never said she had a mother.'

'I know. Doesn't like to.'

'What?'

Dad doesn't give me Mother's usual reply to that question either: 'He invented steam.' He says instead, 'Talk about her. Painful.'

'Why?'

'In a bin.'

A bin – I think – is what Mother puts the tea leaves in, and the outsides of potatoes, and shoes when they crack for good, and all the things we don't need any more.

'In a bin. Her.'

I try to picture Mother's mother in a bin. Dad must be teasing me.

'She lives in a bin?'

'That's it. Not a life I'd like.'

'Smelly.'

'Son?'

'Smelly.'

'Might be. Never visited. Might well be.'

'Is it a bin like ours?'

'Son?'

'Is it kept in the backyard?'

He stops and stares at me. He draws a circle in the air; he pretends that he's throwing something into it; he holds his nose as he slams a lid down. I nod, having recognized his mime. His head goes back and he laughs. It's as if I were Charlie Chaplin or Mickey Mouse.

'Bin!' he shouts. He ruffles my hair. 'Bin!'

I remind him, angrily, that that's where he's told me Mother's mother lives.

'No', he says. 'No, son. No.' He wipes his eyes with the backs of his hands. 'Loony bin. Asylum, Peter. Locked away.' He puts a finger to the side of his head and turns it. 'Round the bend. Cuckoo. Hatter.'

'Bonkers?'

'Mad. Quite young. Husband dead. Shock.'

He takes my hand and presses it. I feel warmth only there, even though it's a hot night; the rest of me is cold.

'Thirsty work. Walking.'

'Yes, Dad.'

'Lemonade?'

'Please, Dad.'

'Pint for Father. Wait, son.'

He goes into the pub. I see Mother speeding towards the bin. To my surprise, I want to join her. I want to know what she calls her mother; what her mother says to her.

I guzzle the lemonade. Dad pours some of his beer into my empty glass. 'Slowly,' he warns. 'Too much. Too quick. Bin.'

I sip. I let my tongue loll and stick my head on my shoulder and make my knees knock together.

'Daft sod. Stand up.'

'Stay like that,' he says when my mad act's over. 'Peter.'

*

21

I saw the Victorian Gothic mansion in which Mrs Dixon lived for nearly thirty years when I was on the run from Nancy's love. Troops of patients were taking exercise in the grounds. I imagined Mother offering them her annual, awkward comfort; and Mrs Dixon—one of that regiment—breaking ranks and curtseying, accepting it (for want of something better) with gratitude. Pure fancy, beneath that appropriate willow: both were dead. I was to know only one of my grandmothers.

Bottles labelled POISON, hands clutching daggers, ridiculously large drops of blood—the covers of Granny Smart's books were as subtle as their contents. To think of *The Ripper Strikes by Night*, *Her Sins Were Scarlet*, *Dead Flesh for Sale* and *She Slashed for Love* is to bring back a happy time. One of the mysteries of my childhood was the fact that Granny, who treated me fondly, should take delight in such brutal stuff; while my mother, always so stern and on occasions positively venomous, never read anything but the soppiest love stories, most of which took place in the Sahara desert.

'If he can find the energy, your father will be taking you to your grandmother's tomorrow. It's a long journey so you'll have to get up early for once, You.'

'Doodlebugs,' said Dad.

'You're going to the country to be out of the way of bombs— that's what he means. That old tramp you'll be staying with is his flesh and blood, not mine. They'll have to cut her out of her underwear when she goes. And don't you ask me why, You.'

I did ask Granny, though, when I was older. 'There's worse things in this world than honest dirt,' was her reply. 'It's better to wear your muck outside than in.'

Granny Smart was waiting on her step for us when the bus stopped in the village's one street. 'You're big enough to do mischief now,' she said, lifting me up to her face. 'It's a long while since I had a man in the house. You can frighten the burglars away for me, can't you?'

She carried me indoors and put me down on a stool by the grate. A large fire blazed there, as it did on every day of the year, regardless of the temperature. On this July afternoon the windows were closed, and as soon as we were all in the parlour the door was shut to, and a heavy rug pushed up against it to keep out draughts. A mug of tea was shoved into my hands by a small, thin woman wearing a threadbare apron – it was so hot that I had to put it aside to cool. 'Your Aunt Hilda,' said Granny, as the woman rushed from the room with her head down. 'She'll notice you when she has a mind to. Cantankerous by nature.'

'Happy Wednesday. Thursday down in dumps,' Dad explained.

'More Thursdays than Wednesdays these days, I reckon, Gerald. Much as I cherished my Bertie, rest his soul, I'd never let any man get a hold on me as Edward Mosford had on her.' She gave me her brown smile. 'Don't you go growing up breaking women's hearts, our Pete. Life's best when it runs easy and natural.'

And it did run easily and naturally whenever I stayed in my brown grandmother's brown house. I emphasize the brownness because I almost came to believe that she doubted the existence of any other colour: her boots, stockings, skirt, blouse; the hat and coat she put on every Christmas Eve to go to church in; the tortoiseshell comb that kept her bun in place – all were brown. Her skin had a brownish tinge, and the flesh between her nose and mouth was rusty from a lifetime's snuff-taking: in the faint light of the oil-lamp it looked like a moustache. She hated falsity in all manifestations, which should explain my reference to her smile. Those stumps were likely to fall out at any time. Whether picked up from the carpet, or fished out of her evening glass of stout, or extricated from a piece of gristle that had caused her gums to bleed, their departure meant nothing to her. They joined her cigarette ends on the ever-blazing fire.

She loomed above her brown surroundings. Unlike my father, who had a passion for vanishing, she never hibernated into the furniture. She could be darker or lighter, but she always stood out, guilelessly. Her anger seemed to spring from a natural source, having nothing in common with Mother's rootless ferocity: I was allowed a glimpse of sun after the thunder.

I hated her at first. Her peculiar smell offended nostrils accustomed to carbolic soap. Mother had been right to call her a tramp. I sat on that wobbly stool and sweated and itched. Wherever I turned my head, some new horror struck me: a grubby antimacassar; a heap of dust in a corner; a stocking full of holes under a chair. Cleanliness was next to Godliness, and the boy who grew up clean would grow up decent: Mother's maxims echoed round Granny's parlour.

I was sent to bed early that night. Sweat still poured from me as Granny led me up to the attic. 'You can't shut that,' said Granny, pointing at the skylight. 'It's only Miladies in their chambers who don't let the fresh air in while they sleep.' She helped me to undress. Each piece of clothing was slung on to the bare floorboards. Dad came in, carrying my pyjamas. 'Gerald Smart, he's not wearing those fancy things in my house. You slept raw as a lad and so will he.'

Even though it was summer, the sheets were icy. I shivered between them. Dad said good night and Granny gave me a beery kiss on the lips. I listened from my Arctic eyrie as they returned to the tropics.

Dad went back to London and tidiness in the morning. I was left to sweat and freeze with two strange women, one of whom continued to ignore me. Two long, miserable days passed before Aunt Hilda made up her mind to speak. 'I met your mother— Gerald's wife,' she said. 'At their wedding. I threw confetti. It was all very nice. Do you love her?'

'Yes.' Of course I loved her: all clean and decent children loved their mothers and fathers.

'That's good. I expect she loves you as well. You're very quiet for a boy. If I'd had a boy for a son, I'd have liked him to have manners.'

'Cut me another slice of cake, our Hilda.'

'Yes, Ma.'

Aunt Hilda took Granny's plate to the scullery. 'We mustn't let her brood, our Peter. If she ever mentions weddings or sons and daughters when I'm not here, just ask her to do something. She soon snaps out of it when her hands are occupied.'

A wink accompanied these mysterious words. Curious to know what it was that Aunt Hilda soon snapped out of, I pressed Granny Smart for an explanation. She would tell me, she said, when I was of an age to understand. She pulled me on to her lap. From that moment, I loved her smell. Snuff and stout, I realize now, meant involvement, the keeping of secrets; not exclusion.

Throughout the day Aunt Hilda busily attended to the business of cleaning. She worked with fierce concentration. She flailed the ancient carpet as if it contained demons instead of dust. The furniture received similar injury from her surprisingly large red hands. Yet when she was finished, the floor looked as dirty as ever, and the chairs and tables had no shine on them. Surveying her achievements, she allowed herself one quick, barely perceptible, smile of satisfaction.

There were no smiles – however fleeting – on Mondays, when Aunt Hilda stabbed the washing with a long stick as it soaked in the tub. My shirts, so white in London, were grey now, almost as grey as the sheets on my bed. My aunt's unique contribution to the art of laundering lay in her ability to wash the dirt *in*. New clothes soon became drab from her sweaty labours in the scullery: things that entered the water looking fresh emerged exhausted. An altruistic Midas, anxious to see his gold converted to its original state, would have found Aunt Hilda of invaluable assistance.

Even when her speech was calm, and her eyes dreamy, those red hands were restless. They darted about in her lap like stranded fish. Deprived of brush or duster, they moved without purpose, as if some madness affected them. They were especially lively at weddings: once, as we were watching a procession leave the church, she asked me in a loud whisper to take hold of them, to keep them in a firm grip.

'They're disgracing me today,' she said. 'They're all of a flutter.'

'Go down to Edna's for my stout, our Hilda. And have him fill the little jug as well.'

Every evening at seven Aunt Hilda went to The Wheatsheaf for Granny's beer.

'You can have a fairy's thimbleful tonight, young man. It'll make the hairs sprout on your chest.'

'Do they grow on yours, Gran?'

'Not yet they don't, our Pete. I'll let you know when I see them coming up.'

'What if I like it? The beer, I mean, Granny.'

'What if you do?'

'Mother says it's bad for people. It sends them cuckoo. She says it's never passed her lips. She says if Dad wants to drink the filthy stuff then he has to do it outside her walls.'

'She's all mouth and trousers, your mother is. She'd give a laughing hyena cause to weep.'

Aunt Hilda came into the parlour with her usual bustle. She placed the two jugs—one very large, the other tiny—on the cluttered sideboard.

'Off with your shirt and vest, our Pete.'

'It's not my bedtime yet.'

'I don't recall saying it was, though my memory might be failing me. You can have your tipple when I've seen those creatures off.'

'Creatures?'

'Lice.'

'What's lice?'

'Lice is a louse multiplied, young man. You've been up at the farm today—I could tell by the smell on you when you walked in for your tea—so I'll send those lice away before they can get started.'

While I undressed, Aunt Hilda filled a bowl with hot water. She put a finger into it, brought it out quickly, and then added cold. When the temperature was considered right, she set the bowl on the table. I was ordered to crouch on a chair and stick my head in the water.

No sooner was my hair immersed than Granny yanked it out. She rubbed my scalp roughly with her horny fingers.

'Pass the jug, our Hilda.'

Granny poured beer over my head.

'Makes the little blighters drunk. They stagger like a Scot on a Saturday when this gets into their systems.'

The ordeal over, I stared into the water. No lice swam drunkenly into view.

And they never did, in all the years I spent in the country. I went to the farm a thousand times and after each visit I was rewarded with a fairy's thimbleful as soon as Granny had sent the lice staggering on their invisible way.

I have yet to meet a louse (of the species Anoplura), but I did meet Death – whose friendship I have sought so vainly, so often – while I lived with Granny. She introduced us.

Or rather, she showed me his handiwork. She told me how wily he was, and crafty; how he got up to tricks with people and took them unawares.

I was nine when she first invited me to go with her on one of her 'special visits'. Aunt Hilda protested mildly before we left the house. She told Granny I was too young to see such things; a child shouldn't have to face horrible sights until he was a man.

'Our Pete has his feet on the ground, our Hilda, not halfway in the air like yours. Seeing me deal with Mr Lovell won't do him much harm.'

So, one autumn morning, I watched my grandmother as she dealt with Mr Lovell. Her way of dealing with him was to wash each part of his body gently and thoroughly. He didn't respond to her gentleness, though I hoped he would. Mrs Lovell was making the ugliest noise I'd ever heard, and I wanted it to stop.

'I said help me turn him over, our Pete. Mrs Lovell's in no fit state to. I'll push him to your side.'

I made a grab for his cold left arm as it came towards me. I held it in a firm grip until it landed safely on the bed.

'He's messed his bum, Gran.'

'It would have been a miracle if he hadn't. Everyone makes a motion at the last.'

Mr Lovell's mess vanished with a few brisk flicks of the cloth.

'God won't welcome him this way round. Let's have him as he was.'

Granny leaned across his body, put one hand on his leg and another on his arm, and pulled. I was told to push.

'He can't feel anything, our Pete. Put some gumption into it.'

One of his eyes had opened. Mrs Lovell screamed.

'I haven't worked a miracle, Amy Lovell, so quiet yourself,' said Granny as she pulled the lid down. 'You can make us all some tea. This minute.'

The sheet Granny Smart covered Mr Lovell with had obviously not been washed by Aunt Hilda.

I thought of Tommy as I waited icily for sleep that night. I saw him unboxed, lying as Mr Lovell had lain, his tiny body still. I wondered who had wiped his cacky bum for him.

I shook my legs, to warm them.

I put Tommy back in his box, and tried to picture the flowers.

'He's got her!'

Granny Smart couldn't contain her enthusiasm when reading. I was able to follow the action by the remarks she made.

'In one bound as well!'

'It always is.'

'What always is, our Hilda?'

'It's always in one bound. Never two or three. Whoever he is, Ma, he always gets her in one bound.'

'I dare say. Don't let me lose my flow. Where was I?'

'You were where he'd got her in one bound, Gran.'

'That's it. Now let me be.'

Then, mumbling something to the effect that people who were occupied themselves shouldn't annoy other people who were occupied differently, she returned to her 'savage tale of a torrid passion that brought foul murder in its wake'.

I stared at my dull comic. Aunt Hilda sat close to the lamp, knitting a jumper that would turn out to be too small for me.

'It serves the silly bitch right!'

The 'silly bitch' was a 'scarlet woman'—a type my brown grandmother had little patience with. The more brutally she was murdered, the louder Granny chuckled.

I hear that laugh now, and it chills me. For the men and women she read about so avidly had once lived, like her. They weren't the stuffed dummies of English detective fiction—old Parkin, the gardener, shot through the heart among his rhododendrons; or cheery Canon Richards, whose mysterious death after Holy Communion sparks off a train of events which leads to the revelation in the closing pages that he was none other than Reichardt, the villainous spy from eastern Europe. No, the 'sticky ends' those sad creatures came to—in the gutter; on the gallows—weren't contrived for entertainment, however diverting Granny Smart found them. They took place.

It would please me to write that her laughter signified disbelief. I can't, though: she knew it was all true. If a woman sold her body, then she was beyond pity—my warm grandmother had been taught as a child to put her faith in some cold doctrines. For her, a crime wasn't a crime unless sex was involved. If she was smiling when Aunt Hilda and I came back from church on Sunday, it was because her favourite newspaper had printed some particularly juicy stories. Sometimes she would be glowering—'Nothing but bloody robberies this week.'

Perhaps I shouldn't examine too closely—and with the useless advantage of hindsight—the mentality of a simple-minded, kind old woman. As I've said, the lurid covers of her books bring back a happy time to me. The act of writing about her—of paying her the homage that is her due—has forced me to consider what reasons lay behind her need (for she read voraciously) to follow to their predictably squalid ends the unfortunate adventures of those who had been brought low by love.

Granny Smart was no saint, and I am a middle-aged prig. Let me consider her brusque kindness instead; it is worth the effort. An outsider, seeing her at ease in her brown surroundings while her daughter dusts here and polishes there or merely stands still with her hands in a commotion, would soon decide that Matilda Smart was a slave-driver and Hilda a drudge. It was a view of their relationship I often heard expressed in the village.

Aunt Hilda's senseless drudgery didn't make sense to me until the summer of my father's death. I'd come to the country for my holidays. Late one night, Granny and I were left together in the tropics. She reminded me of the promise she'd made years before: I was old enough now, in my long trousers, to understand. My poor aunt, she told me, had once made a cock-eyed fool of herself. She'd fallen head over heels, or arse over tip—

depending how you looked at it—for a man called Edward Mosford.

'Bertie and me, we put no trust in him. He was smooth as a babe's cheek. When he sent a smile your way, you could see the clock in his brain keeping a check on the time of it.'

Aunt Hilda, Granny said, had been swept off her feet, and nothing short of marriage would make the blessed things land smack on the earth again. Love, if that was the proper word for her state of mind, had brought out a will in the girl, a determination. She'd screamed and stamped whenever so much as a single word was spoken against her beloved Edward. Like a knight in shining armour, he was; he could do no wrong.

'A handsome blighter, and that's the truth of it. There's a photo of him in the second album from the bottom in the top right-hand drawer of the sideboard. I keep it well hidden from her. She'd be mooning over it every minute if I didn't. Fetch it out, our Pete.'

'Is this him?' I pointed to the only handsome face in the entire album.

'How did you know?'

'I guessed, Gran.'

'That's him. Look at his curls. It's a good likeness.'

'What's happened to him?'

'You'll have to ask the Almighty, or Edward Mosford. He could be six feet under, or prospering, for all I could tell you. One thing's as sure as daylight, our Pete: if the sod put his head round that door this minute, your aunt would soon have her bags packed to go off with him again.'

'Did she run away with him?'

'That she did. No farther than Portsmouth, but that's far enough when you're young and daft. Bertie and me would have let them marry when they'd both calmed down a bit, but our Hilda couldn't wait. Off she went with her fancy man, leaving your grandfather and me none the wiser as to where she was heading.'

So Aunt Hilda had been, in her unflamboyant way, a 'scarlet woman' of sorts. Passion had claimed her. After a few months of unmarried bliss in a boarding-house, Edward Mosford told her he was leaving for Australia. He would find a job and make a pile of money, and when he had saved sufficient he would send for her and life would be rosy. To no one's surprise but Hilda's, he never sent for her. Not long after his departure, she gave birth to a still-born child – a boy.

'Did she come home?'

'Her pride wouldn't let her. Bertie found her. I think he had some notion that he wasn't long for this world. He wanted to see his daughter happy before he left it. He was only away three days. She was still in Portsmouth, cleaning hospital floors to keep herself alive. There's another of my teeth gone. Oh, she's cantankerous. She turns life into an obstacle race, and says it's what God wants for her.'

'Why does she say that, Gran?'

'If you asked her straight, she'd tell you it's between her and her maker. God meant her little boy to come out dead – that's what she believes. As punishment for her sins.' She stopped and listened. Then she whispered: 'Go and unlatch the stair door quietly. I heard a noise just then. She might be having a pry.'

I peered up the stairs.

'Is the coast clear?'

'Yes, Gran.'

'It must have been somebody's ghost.'

I returned to my stool.

'Do you want a sip of my special?'

'Yes, please, Gran.'

'Drink it out of this, then – it won't poison you. And if it does, it's all in the family. Don't go swallowing the tooth, will you?'

I didn't. I spat it on to the fire.

'You forgot to ask me if I wanted it back.'

We laughed.

'I'd be happy to do the work around the place. Well, as much of it as my body will take.' She whispered once more: 'And, I'm afraid to say, I'd do it a damned sight better. She goes at it with such a will, I couldn't bear to stop her – it would hurt her so. She doesn't expect thanks. So long as I leave her be to storm away every morning, she's content.' She added, after a considerable silence: 'As content as a soul can be who's had a corpse come out of her and a man unfaithful.'

She put down her glass and clapped her hands and said this was no way to talk to a young man with a whole life ahead of him.

'Thank God, our Pete, God didn't order Hilda to do the cooking too. Then the lot of us would have been punished.'

Shortly after noon the next day the telegram came.

My mother shed a tear once. It rolled down her cheek on a winter's evening.

Some while before it appeared, she had been in her customary bad temper. Mr Attlee, like Mr Churchill ahead of him, was leading the country to rack and ruin. One day, she said, she would smash the wireless in two: it brought her no pleasure; the politicians saw to that.

'You' had switched it off when she'd ordered him to.

'I shall settle myself with a story.'

For an hour or more, F. Leonard Cottie's kitchen was blessed with a rare quiet, while 'You' did further research into the subject that wouldn't get him far in the here and now, and Mother peered over her glasses at the book she was holding at arm's length.

I noticed Mother's tear when the doctor rang for service. It left a trail behind as it descended. She pulled off her glasses, and rubbed all trace of it away.

'What can he want this late? He's practised his bedside manner already today.'

Despite the fact that she must have reached the second-floor landing, I went on tiptoe to her chair. I wanted to know what had made her cry.

The book, I remember, was about the love affair between a young aristocrat, Sir Eustace, and a green-eyed servant girl, Imelda. So deep and abiding was his affection for the spirited little colleen that he had defied his father, Lord Delford, and refused to marry the Honourable Lavinia. Disowned by his family, he had no choice but to join the Foreign Legion.

Eustace's poignant farewell to Imelda had prompted Mother's tear:

'Thousands of miles will separate us, and the desert sun will bronze my skin with its fierce rays, and the rough male company of my fellow legionaries will be my only diversion, but— Imelda'— a sob caught in the nobleman's throat—'my heart will call to yours across those wastes. You, my precious girl, will be my oasis.'

The knowledge increased my dismay. I returned to Oliver Cromwell. He was within my understanding.

There was an apple tree in the garden behind Granny's house. One December morning it bore strange fruit.

I awoke in the dark with a pain in my stomach and an urgent need to do the one thing that would cure it. But so strong was my fear of the pitch black outside that I lay rigid in bed with the sides of my bum pressed together and prayed that I wouldn't have an accident. I would make the long journey to the privy as soon as it was light.

Nature decided otherwise. The pain became unbearable and the prospect of a violent explosion inevitable. I pulled on my trousers and somehow got my vest over my head. My progress down the stairs, through the scullery and along the garden path was agonizingly slow—with cheeks so tightly held together, I had to move one leg at a time, wait, and then move the other one. Only when I was on the seat did I realize that the wicked people who came out at night had left me alone. I hadn't been pounced upon or tied up in a sack—I pinched my arm to make sure. It hurt. I was all in one piece.

A new day dawned as I sat there.

On the way back to the house, I noticed a man's shoe among the cabbages. I picked it up—the leather was cracked and the sole hung loose. I searched for its partner, and discovered it eventually under the rose bush. It too was beyond repair.

The feet they belonged to dangled in front of me. At the top of a skinny body in scarecrow clothes—ragged trousers gone at

33

the knees; a striped shirt full of holes – was a purple face from which blue eyes bulged. I glimpsed thick rope beneath it. I saw cropped blond hair and thought of the wheat fields after harvest.

Siegfried Günter Schmidt, an escaped prisoner of war from the camp in the castle grounds, was cut down that same day. He was carried through the parlour. Everyone in the village watched as he was slung into the back of a truck and taken off for ever.

'You look like an animal, You. You can start taming yourself now you're back among respectable people. I don't know what that aunt of yours on your father's side does to your shirts but whatever it is it's about as useful as washing them in soot.'

I have come home for Christmas.

'You don't smell very fresh either. Your father will run a bath for you when he can summon the energy to get up out of his chair. The war will probably be over by the time that happens. Oh look, he's taken the hint. Wonders will never cease. You're a disgrace to me, You. If a bomb fell this minute and you were hit, the whole street would see the state of your vest and pants and my name would be mud, if it isn't that already.'

I emerge from the bath with my skin raw from her scrubbing.

'You look like a son of mine again, You. All I hope is that Hitler gets what's due to him before January's here. Then you won't have to go back to that tramp of a grandmother on your father's side and that person she's proud to call her daughter – which is something I wouldn't call her if I'd given her breath.'

'Your Mum's got a terrible cough, Peter.'

'Shall we have a game of cards, Bobby?'

'It must be the one I had last month. They go from person to person. If my mouth is open and I've got a cold and I'm in the same room as your Mum and she's got her mouth open as well, then the germs I've got go out of my mouth and into her mouth.'

'Shall I show you my film-star photos, Bobby?'

'If my Mum and my Dad knew that your Mum had a terrible cold and that I was here when she had it, they wouldn't have let me come.'

'We can listen to the wireless if you want.'

'If I get another one and have to miss school like I did last month then I'll have to tell the doctor that your Mum's germs passed into my mouth when she opened the door to me the night I went round to Peter Smart's house.'

'What about dominoes?'

'Germs move very quickly. That's why so many people are ill. I should have worn my scarf tonight. I could have had it round my mouth when your Mum let me in.'

'Snakes and ladders, Bobby?'

'My Mum says I have to look after myself, with my weak chest. She says if anything should happen to my Dad I would be all she had left in the world. There's your Mum coughing again. She sounds terrible. I couldn't live here; I really couldn't.'

The perpetually worried Bobby Shorter – a skinny old man of eleven when this conversation, or monologue with interruptions, took place – need not have upset himself: Mother's cough was pure artifice; a dazzling impersonation of the real thing. Death seemed imminent when she was on form, as she was that night. I didn't tell Bobby that her coughing fits were perpetrated to cover the noise another part of her body was making at the same time. In the final year of my father's life, and for many years following, my mother had trouble with her wind. A long, rasping cough signified great disorder below; a genteel 'Er-hum' indicated a mild disturbance. The first cough of the evening, which came soon after our meal, was called 'the gale warning' by my father.

'Not supposed to.'

'What, Dad?'

'Fart. Ladies. Only men. Why she chokes herself.'

'Some friends you choose,' said my mother after Bobby Shorter's first and last visit to our house. 'What a pipsqueak. I know food's rationed, but he looks as if he's never eaten any. And the way he kept his hand over his mouth when I came into the room! You steer clear of him, You. He's a bad influence if ever I saw one.'

I had tried steering clear of him already, but to no avail. Bobby Shorter had sought me out for friendship. I was the chosen one.

For no discernible reason, he had to go everywhere with me: I couldn't even pee without him. He spoke to no one else; no other boy was kept informed of his illnesses, and the amazing recoveries that were contingent upon them. I lacked the courage to tell him that he bored and embarrassed me.

The invitation to come to our house was extended out of kindness. Or pity, perhaps: I suppose I wanted to show him he was welcome somewhere. Welcome! Not only did he not respond to the delights of 67 Ranley Road, they actually inspired him to a new awareness of his own frailty. Disconsolate on arrival, he left us in a state of total dejection.

Thanks to Mother's bravura performance, Bobby Shorter began to avoid me at school. I peed alone. He tried attaching himself to another boy, but was quickly and firmly repulsed. This failure did not deter him, however: a more tolerant substitute, 'Fatty' Wale, became the special sharer of Bobby's woes. Because they looked so absurd together they were nicknamed Laurel and Hardy.

I was surprised by my feelings when Bobby abandoned me. I was unhappy for weeks. I missed his joyless company, the smell of his pepperminty breath. Then annoyance replaced unhappiness —annoyance that someone like *him* had cast aside someone like *me*.

My father vanished for good. I put away childish things. The world darkened, and so did I.

'You won't need these where you're going, You.' Mother slung my film-star photographs from Culver City, U.S.A., into the dustbin. My comics soon joined them. I made no protest. 'Dr Cottie's an intelligent man. I don't want you showing me up with these silly things.'

'I don't want them any more.'

'Will I be glad to get this place behind me? I'll say I will. I shan't be happy until tomorrow dawns and we can say ta-ta to Ranley Road and everyone in it. You'll have to buck yourself up from now on, you will, You. No more lying in bed every morning while your poor mother's at her wit's end trying to keep your breakfast warm. No. The young lord and master will have to drag his carcass out of the sheets a damned sight earlier than he's been used to doing, because making his way over here to school will mean an hour on the bus from where he'll be living after tonight. Oh, yes.'

'You don't have to shout, Mother.'

'I'll shout if I want to without asking your permission, You. You can tell there isn't a man in the house – you wouldn't answer me back if there was.'

'Where does this Dr So-and-so live?'

'His name isn't So-and-so, You, it's Cottie. Dr F. Leonard Cottie. And for your information, he lives in Kensington. Yes, Kensington. We'll be living in a respectable district at last.'

The doctor's house in the oppressively quiet cul-de-sac was called The Elms. There were no elm trees nearby. Each morning during the school term I left it for the liveliness of Lambeth. At week-ends, and in the long holidays, I read.

F. Leonard Cottie's library became my favourite place on earth. There seemed to be no limit to the treasures it contained. The books I studied under the guidance of my teacher, Mr Campbell, weren't enough for me: I needed more information, more surprises, more people. I found them in that large room on the first floor, outside which Sebastian the skeleton kept permanent guard.

It was in there that I first made the acquaintance of the Prince of Denmark.

I don't want to write about my involvement with Hamlet yet. Our deep relationship will be accounted for at a later stage in this haphazard narrative. Meanwhile, my mother's solid flesh has appeared to me.

'Have you been up in Dr Cottie's library again?'

'Yes.'

'Filling your head with ideas!'

'Don't you want me to be intelligent?'

'Intelligent, yes. But not to have your head filled with ideas out of books.'

'I don't understand.'

'I speak plain English. I know what I mean. If you don't follow me, you must have a screw coming loose.'

'I don't understand how I can be intelligent without having ideas.'

'I do.'

'Tell me then.'

'There's ideas—' She stares at me and nods slowly. '—and there's ideas.'

'What's the difference between them?'

'You'll find out.' Her voice rises to a shriek. 'You'll find out! One of these fine days!'

'When?'

'A wen's a nasty swelling.' She savours her wit with a harsh little laugh. 'You ask him upstairs.'

'I was asking you, Mother.'

'I'm too busy to answer your questions, You.'

'But you're not doing anything.'

'How do you know?'

'I'm looking at you.'

'Were you reading his medical books?'

'No.'

'I should hope not. All those details.'

'Which details?'

'The ones you'll find out about in the right time and place and not before because it's not natural.'

'What isn't natural?'

'You'll find out.'

'How long will I have to wait?'

'Saved by the bell!' The doctor is ringing for service. 'I'm going up to satisfy his requirements.' She smiles. 'Goodness, there's crumbs on my shelf,' she says, brushing away the remains of a biscuit from her bosom.

We were sitting down to a meal in the tropics when the telegram came. Granny Smart took it from the boy and shoved it into the cardigan pocket where she kept her snuff-box.

'You'd best read it,' said the boy. 'In case a reply's called for.'

She lit a cigarette shakily. Then she plumped up the cushions in her chair. She settled herself slowly. She said, 'You never know, it might be good news. Miracles happen sometimes.'

Aunt Hilda whispered loudly to me: 'Take hold of my hands, Peter. Oh, just look at them! He hasn't noticed, has he?'

The boy smiled.

'No.'

'I hate strangers seeing.'

Granny read the message.

'No bloody miracle.'

'Is a reply called for?'

'Yes. "On our way. Matilda." '

' "On our way. Matilda." '

She gave the boy some coins. 'Get drunk with the change.' He thanked her and left.

She threw the cigarette on to the fire.

The sweat had dried on me. I shivered. I ended the silence by saying: 'It's Dad.'

'Yes. Our Gerald's ill.'

'Not dead?'

She stood up and shouted: 'No, you miserable bugger, he's not. There's breath in him yet. Don't send him off before he's due.'

'No, Ma. You mustn't. The boy's gone like ice.'

Granny continued to shout: 'Our Gerald's going to do what Bertie did. There's no bloody fight in him either. His mind's on Kingdom Come already. The sod. The sod won't put up a battle.'

'Let me have my hands back, Peter.'

I did as Aunt Hilda asked. I sensed that she had a use for them. She went to her mother and embraced her.

'Ma, quiet yourself.'

'You're a fine one to talk of quiet. You never rest.'

'That's me, not you.'

'The spineless sod.'

'No, Ma. He's not. No, Ma.'

Granny put her arms round Hilda.

'I'll get my case ready,' I said.

'Yes, young man, you do.'

'Fold your clothes tidy, Peter.'

When I came down from the attic, Granny was back in her chair, sipping beer.

'There's a glass for you on the table, our Pete. Hilda's just packing Milady's valise. We'll be off shortly.'

The foul taste of Granny's 'medicine' stayed with me on the journey to London. I wondered, as we both looked out at the passing countryside, if she saw the same long shadow blackening the green landscape. For me, it was a constant presence. It had its own substantiality; it was independent of trees or houses or telegraph poles. It fought with the mellow sunlight. By the time the train reached Waterloo, it was the undoubted victor.

'Where is he?' My mother was still opening the front door when Granny pushed past her. 'It seems like a hundred years ago since I was last in here.'

'Up the stairs.'

'What's wrong with him?'

'The doctor says it's pneumonia.'

'It's a daft time of year to have that complaint. If he's got pneumonia, why isn't he in hospital?'

'The doctor said to wait and see.'

'That's what most doctors do, I've found. When they've got through waiting and seeing, there's nothing left to cure. It's all over, bar the burying.'

'He was calling for you in his sleep.'

'The doctor?'

'No. Him.'

'I know who it was. I just fancied hearing my son's name on your lips for once.'

'Gerald's in here, Mrs Smart.'

'I'll see him alone for a moment or so. If that's convenient.'

'Of course it's convenient, Mrs Smart. No trouble at all.'

Granny's 'moment or so' lasted more than an hour. She joined us in the 'best' room. It was only opened when we had visitors. It had a musty smell.

'You can do two things for me, Ellen.'

40

'And what are they, Mrs Smart?'

'First you can tell your quack there's been enough waiting and seeing. Gerald needs moving to the hospital.'

'I can't tell *the doctor* just like that, Mrs Smart.'

'Yes you bloody well can. Don't play little Miss Helpless with me, because I know your nature like I know my own. Since when have you found that you can't give an order?'

Mother's expression, straining towards humility, suggested that she had rarely been paid such a compliment.

'What's the second thing, Mrs Smart?'

'The second thing, Ellen, you'll disapprove of, but that can't be helped. If I'm staying in this house, I shall be wanting my creature comforts. The demon drink, in other words.'

'You must treat the place like home, Mrs Smart.'

'Must I? I don't expect you to go into a pub for me, but if you could tell me where the nearest one is —'

'You're an old woman — lady, Mrs Smart. I'll be happy to fetch your beer for you.'

'Thank you, Ellen. I'm obliged. Now I'm thinking, as you're so young and fit, that you should run round and knock the doctor up.'

'You know where Dr Pashley lives, You.' Turning to me, she sweetened her tone. 'Go and tell him your father's taken a turn for the worse. You don't mind going, do you, Peter?'

'No, Mother.'

'You're a good son.'

When I returned with the news that the ambulance would be coming at nine, Mother affirmed her recently discovered belief in my goodness. 'Go and sit with your grandmother at the bedside, there's a good boy. I'll cook something light for us, though I doubt if we'll be able to find an appetite for food tonight.'

The colour of his skin was the first thing I noticed. His face had a greenish tinge. His mouth opened and shut as he slept: it was as if he were biting air into it. Then he smiled briefly and said, 'Alice'.

'Who's Alice, Gran?'

'Sh. Not so loud. Where's Mouth and Trousers? I mean, where's your mother?'

'In the kitchen.'

'Open the door a fraction and make sure.'

I peeped out.

'I can hear her. She's cooking.'

'Alice was the girl our Gerald was all set to marry when he got home from Flanders. She died of a burst appendix. It broke his heart.'

'She's dead, Gran?'

'Well, if she was living you wouldn't be standing here inquiring if she was dead, now would you? Gerald would have married her and our Pete would never have seen the light of day. Just imagine.'

He said the name again when the two men were taking him downstairs on the stretcher.

He opened his eyes. He stared at me.

'Dad.'

'I bet those bloody Boche aren't eating bully beef from arsehole to breakfast.'

He snorted and went back to sleep.

The ambulance doors closed on him.

'It happens,' said my grandmother while we were trying to eat the meal Mother had left for us.

'What happens?'

'At the end. They go back in their minds. If he wakes up, he won't see her. He'll have his Alice looking down at him.'

'He didn't recognize me.'

'I know, child. He saw me for barely a second when I was in there with him. I said my goodbyes. No more palaver now. He's gone from us.'

'You could have washed him,' I heard myself say.

'Not my own kind, our Pete. Oh, no. Strangers, yes – they're bound up, once they've passed, with other people's misery. I'm not as tough as I care to think. I couldn't have done it for him. They'll cope at the Bethel.'

And cope they did, but not to my mother's satisfaction. The nurses, she told us the next evening, were a hard-hearted lot who showed no respect for a widow's feelings. The cup of tea they brought to calm her nerves when her poor, dear Gerald breather his last was hot water dyed light brown: if she hadn't been in such a state, she would have given them her opinion of it.

'No wonder everyone says that place is like a butcher's. My poor, dear Gerald was hardly gone before they were wheeling him out. They think you're just flesh and nothing else.'

'The Almighty looks after our souls, Ellen. Our Gerald's is in safe hands, if that's what's bothering you.'

'They did it while I was there, Mrs Smart — that's what upsets me. I was given no time at all to recover.'

'Weren't you?'

'You could see they wanted to be rid of me. I would have kicked up a fuss, only it didn't seem right in the circumstances. The nurse who showed me the way out was almost pushing me.'

'Perhaps it was a busy night.'

'Not that *I* saw.'

'With your feelings in such a state, Ellen, I shouldn't think you were able to see very much.'

'Of course. Of course not, Mrs Smart.'

'How's that cough of yours?'

'Not so bad. Oh, not so bad.'

'I've cooked a pie for us with some nice bits of stewing lamb. I hope your stomach can take it, Ellen.'

'What's my cough got to do with my stomach?' Mother screamed. 'Some people's minds!'

'I swear I've no idea what it has to do with it, Ellen. Grief's playing funny tricks with you.'

'Yes, it must be. It was silly of me to explode like that.'

'You'll feel better once you've eaten.'

How wrong Granny was. Mother's second explosion that evening was considerably more alarming than the first. It began as a rumble.

'There's something in my mouth.'

Granny smiled at her pityingly. 'It's the pie, Ellen.'

'There's something in the pie and it's in my mouth.'

'I can't hear you properly. Tell me when you've swallowed your food.'

'Swallow! Do you think I'm going to swallow?'

'You've turned purple —'

'There it is! There it is!'

The object she spat out clinked as it hit the plate. Her rage increased when she realized what it was.

'It's a tooth!'

'You've lost a tooth, Ellen?'

'Not me! You!'

'Me?'

'It's one of yours!'

'It could be. It could well be. They fall out of my face, and I hardly notice they've gone sometimes. Thank the Lord they don't give me pain any more. The little blighters don't bother with a warning now before they drop.'

'The damage! Just think of the damage!'

'I'm too old to miss them—'

'The damage to me! If that dirty-looking thing had got into my gullet and blocked it up, I might have choked to death.'

'Stop talking daft, Ellen.'

'Don't call me Ellen.'

'What shall I call you then?'

'You show me respect.'

'I am—'

'Calling me Ellen and trying to choke me—a fine way to treat a woman who has lost her husband.'

'You need to rest. You've the funeral to face.'

'I'd have been in the box with him if it wasn't for the fact that I always chew carefully. The damage!'

'You're doing damage to our eardrums, Ellen, so stop that bloody caterwauling this minute. I've lost a son and he's lost a father and you've lost your senses, and if you don't want a bucket of cold water over your head I'd advise you to get them back.'

Mother rose from the table.

'You're a good son, Peter,' she said. 'No mother could ask for a better.'

The peck my right ear received from her lips was the first kiss I can remember her giving me. It was definitely the last.

'Is the little boy's drum better now?'

'Yes, Mother.'

'I'm so glad. Good night, Mrs Smart. Your stomach should be grateful my teeth aren't loose.'

She closed the door quietly behind her.

On the day of the funeral, Mother's grief was given dulcet expression. After the burial, she thanked the few mourners for their beautiful floral tributes and reminded them of my father's virtues: men like her poor, dear Gerald were rare. He'd kept his light under a bushel, but it had shone just the same. It was against her nature to contradict a clever man like the doctor, but it was her view that the Blighty wound Gerald got while fighting for his king and country was the cause of his early death. It had taken its toll; oh yes, it had taken it, slowly but surely.

I wept as I said goodbye to Granny and Aunt Hilda on the platform at Waterloo. I grabbed my aunt's hands to still them, and to give myself support as well—I had sensed, on the way to the station, that something more than the two women was leaving me. They were taking my childhood away with them.

'Think of us now and then, our Pete.'

'Don't let your mother make you forget us,' said my aunt sternly. 'Not that you will. God strike me for trying to turn a son against his mother, who it's his duty to love, but don't let her, Peter.'

'Of course I won't forget you.'

'There's no such thing as "of course" in this world, our Pete. I've learnt one lesson from life, and that's it.'

'London's worse than Portsmouth for strangers, Ma. Give me my hands back, Peter. We'd best be on the train before the whistle goes.'

'Dry your eyes, young man.'

I waved to them from the barrier with the dirty handkerchief Granny had given me to do so.

I walked in the opposite direction to home. I sat on a bench by the Thames and thought of the tears I had recently shed. They had sprung up, in an embarrassing abundance, from some source I was unable to name.

I can name it now. Indeed, I was able to name it in my youth, when the feeling that I had been deserted changed for a time into a conviction. Loneliness had warned me of its arrival in my life, causing me to clutch at the slippery security of Aunt Hilda's hands.

'Where have you been, You? What does the clock say?'

'Half-past ten.'

'And that woman's train left at five. You're getting to be like your father, You—always absent when there's work to be done.'

'Perhaps I'm hiding my light under a bushel.'

'I've cleaned this house from top to bottom. Insects queue up to breed on that woman, I'm certain of it.'

The smell of disinfectant was overpowering.

'And as for that creature she's proud to call her daughter—'

'Which is something you wouldn't call her—'

'If *I'd* given her breath, no I wouldn't. She could have stuffed her hands into her pockets at the graveside for decency's sake, I must say. I swear no one looked at the coffin.'

'I did.'

It was 'You' who was then dismissed to bed. Peter's brief candle had been snuffed out.

Mother bought a new pair of shoes to celebrate her appointment as F. Leonard Cottie's housekeeper. They were made of imitation crocodile and were far too small for her. They would only be worn, she said as she forced her feet into them on the morning of our departure from Ranley Road, on 'special occasions'.

The noise they made when she started walking had more in common with the squeak of the rodent than the snap of the crocodile. She seemed to be treading on mice. Their cries accompanied us along the street, and ceased—apart from the odd whimper when she crossed her legs—once we had taken our places on the bus. They began again as we approached The Elms. That short stretch of road was a Via Dolorosa. The creatures didn't achieve their eternal rest until Mother and I were left alone in the doctor's spacious kitchen. The shoes came off, and so did the furious smile which Mother had adopted to disguise the pain they caused her.

'You can mend your ways now we're here, You. You saw

what a gentleman Dr Cottie is. Your Lambeth and country manners won't do for him. You can watch how you talk to me, too. If he catches you being rude to your mother, he'll soon put you in your place, never you fear.'

'Yes, Mother.'

'I've longed all my life to live like this. Oh, there'll be some changes now!'

She was right.

Under the Doctor

A visit to the local market always lifts my spirits. In need of a
respite from these confessions, I went there this morning. The
liveliness of the place soon cheered me: voluminous ladies' underwear, garishly coloured, flapped in the breeze, adding to the
atmosphere of carnival. While I was watching pink bloomers
billow, the man who specializes in foreign finches called me over
to his shop. I looked exactly the type of gentleman, he assured
me, who would be pleased to relieve him of a home-sick toucan
at a bargain price. With Fu Manchu's likely return in mind, I
refused his offer.

I bought asparagus at one stall, figs at another. When my bag
was filled with enough fruit and vegetables to last me a week, I
went to browse at Mr Grimley's book store. Ignoring the piles of
grubby paperbacks, I scanned the shelves at the rear. There was a
single point of brightness in that tired array: the blue and gold
spine of an imposing volume. It looked familiar, that spine. I put
on my dark glasses and peered. Pressed between *Through Dante's
Land* by Mrs Colquhoun Grant and *A Classified List of Registered
Chartered Accountants in England and Wales — 1923 Edition* was a
pristine copy of *With Stethoscope and Scalpel: The Memoirs of a
Physician and Surgeon* by F. Leonard Cottie, M.D., F.R.C.S.

'I can tell you're a connoisseur.'

'Are you talking to me?'

'Who else?' Dusty Mr Grimley was at my side. 'I can see
which one you have your eye on.'

'I'll buy it,' I said.

'You're wise. It's not just a book, it's an investment.'

I took some coins from my pocket.

'Ten pounds, if you please.'

'Ten pounds!'

'And worth every penny. It's the name inside that makes it so costly.'

I asked whose name it was as I wrote out the cheque.

'Albert Einstein.'

Every one of my thirteen copies of the Cottie memoirs is inscribed to a famous person. I shall list this diverse bunch of luminaries in alphabetical order: Fred and Adele Astaire (the only duo, to my knowledge, to be so honoured), Feodor Chaliapin, Winston Churchill, Noël Coward, Alexander Fleming, Henry Ford, Greta Garbo, Radclyffe Hall, the Aga Khan, Pablo Picasso, Albert Schweitzer, Jan Sibelius and Arturo Toscanini. I have yet to see a copy without an inscription on its fly-leaf.

' "To that mighty pioneer, Albert Einstein. A small token of esteem from a humble medic. In boundless admiration. F. Leonard Cottie" ', I read. For that heartfelt message, Mr Grimley had deprived me of ten pounds.

'I knew him,' I said.

'You knew Einstein?'

'No. Cottie.'

Mr Grimley looked unimpressed. 'Oh.' After a silence, he asked with a polite lack of interest who 'this Cottie' was.

I replied, inadequately, that he was a strange old man who once lived in a vast house in Kensington, and had left me some money in his will.

'Have you read this book then?'

'Dozens of times.'

'You must enjoy it.'

'I do. It's appalling, but I do.'

'I've only read one book twice in my entire life, and that was *Clarissa*.'

'The doctor's autobiography', I said with some confidence, 'is not quite in the same class.'

With Stethoscope and Scalpel was published in 1936 by Messrs Askew and Machin of 3 Felix Court, off Paternoster Row,

London, EC4. Since this building had its foundations in the consistently frustrated fantasy life of its two 'owners', it is hard to discover how Dr Cottie got in touch with them. The subsequent addresses of David Askew and Norman Machin—Pentonville, Wormwood Scrubs and, latterly, Wakefield—I have found no difficulty in locating.

One other book bears their imprint: a collection of poems called *Lo! The Trestles!* Its author was a nun named Sister Evangeline. Before taking the veil in her late forties, Evangeline had been the most successful whore in Europe, with several royal persons and assorted financiers among her clients. Publishing Evangeline's poetic effusions was something of a scoop for Askew and Machin: even my grandmother, to whom the names Keats and Tennyson meant nothing, had heard of *her*. Unlike the doctor's more substantial volume, *Lo! The Trestles!* sold well.

I encountered Evangeline's poems comparatively late in life. Her book, a *succès de scandale* at the time of its publication, became a collector's item in the nineteen fifties. It took the British Museum a whole decade to find a replacement copy after the war. My own long search came to an end in Edinburgh, where I was hiding from Nancy. I paid a shilling for it.

The cover Askew and Machin designed for *Lo! The Trestles!* is stunningly clever. On the front, beneath the title, a nun stands at the convent gates—a gaunt figure photographed in a snowstorm; on the back, the *louche* Evangeline of yesteryear, champagne glass in hand, beams blearily as a diamond bracelet is secured to her outstretched arm by a Balkan prince rendered almost maniacal by lust. With the aid of a powerful magnifying glass, and a photo of Machin leaving the Central Criminal Court, I was able to identify that surprisingly strong-jawed nun posing among the snowflakes, who bore absolutely no resemblance to the nubile creature at the prince's table.

Sister Evangeline's poems have nothing of that startling memorability.

> *As through Life's Mire I so fleet of Foot*
> *Past Eden made my solitary Way ...*

makes more sense than most of her stuff. The quotation comes from 'At Peace—April 20, Eastbourne': the second line, with its allusion to a work more certain of survival than her own, suggests that her mind was not inactive during the years of dissoluteness. A cynic might discover, scattered here and there, glancing references to her earlier self. From 'Towards the Gates—October 9, Juan-les-Pins':

> *So must I come? Then come I must ...*

Or this, from 'God's Thunder—August 16, Florence':

> *O that commanding Clap afflicts me still ...*

Only in the totally impenetrable title poem (undated and unplaced) did she display the influence of Modernism:

> *Lo! The Trestles!*
> *Vessels*
> *of Desire!*
> *O Lo!*

Askew and Machin, convinced that Sister Evangeline was too involved with her devotions to concern herself with anything so mundane as money, spent her royalties flamboyantly. They were seen at every social gathering, always accompanied by budding poetesses. Their faith in the nun's gullibility proved to be misplaced.

According to contemporary reports, Sister Evangeline made a striking impression in the courtroom. She played her part well. A golden-hearted prostitute ('All my life I have supported charities') who has slept with royalty ('Even the noblest gentlemen have their moments of blazing passion') and who has renounced a sinful existence ('The thought of it now, Your Honour, fills me with shame') for one of sacrifice ('Once the strain of this trial is over, I shall return to my sisters and my new life') cannot fail with the English public—such a combination of sentimentality, prurient snobbishness and lip-service to religion can usually be guaranteed to stir their hearts. When the

51

defending counsel for Askew and Machin asked her what use she would have put her profits to, she replied, 'To fortify the Church against sin'. The judge said that he had never heard such an inspiring answer. Later in his career, he described an illiterate young murderer from the East End of London as being 'all too typical of his class'.

Askew and Machin were found guilty and sentenced. Sister Evangeline did not continue with her interrupted devotions. She underwent a second conversion. She died in Berlin in 1943.

After our removal to The Elms, I forgot my father for a time. He was even absent from my dreams. Siegfried Günter Schmidt appeared in those, hanging from an apple tree in blossom. He wore smart clothes now. His face was white, and his deep-set blue eyes shone with happiness. The rope remained around his neck. He smiled when he saw me. I smiled back at him. He beckoned me to his side.

I never reached him. I would always wake up with the branch barely inches out of my grasp.

'Mother, what does the "F" stand for?'

'What are you on about, You?'

'The "F" in F. Leonard Cottie—what does it stand for?'

'I can think of a word,' she said with a smirk, 'but I can't recall it ever being used as a Christian name.'

'What word's that?'

'Do you expect me to soil my lips by talking filth? In front of a boy as well? You watch yourself, You. You'll have a mind like a sewer before too long if you don't take care.'

The doctor himself was equally unhelpful.

'My "F"? Aha.' I waited for the revelation. 'Mm. Aha.' He tapped the tip of his nose with his little finger and went upstairs. On the landing, he shook hands with Sebastian and said 'Aha.'

Sebastian, I remember, was the subject of my first real conversation with the doctor. Months before I found the courage to ask him about his 'F', he called to me as I was leaving for school one morning:

'Can you spare a moment?'

'Yes, sir.'

'Are you going willingly or unwillingly?'

'Sir?'

'To school?'

'Willingly.'

'Aha.'

'Do you want me to come upstairs, sir?'

'I should be obliged if you did.'

I joined him on the landing.

'I wish to effect an introduction.'

'To who, sir?'

'Whom.'

'To whom, sir?'

He pointed at the skeleton, standing guard outside his library.

'To him.'

'To him, sir?'

'To him. Take his hand.'

'Which one, sir?'

'Which hand is it customary to take when one is being introduced to a person?'

'The right one, sir.'

'Precisely so.'

I put the skeleton's right hand in mine.

'Sebastian, meet Master Smart.'

'How do you do?' I said, and blushed with embarrassment.

'Isn't he magnificent? The great Leonardo da Vinci, contemplating these bones, would have seen the man they once were part of. Can you see him?'

'No, sir.'

'I was present at his dissection. His kidneys were without pareil.'

'How did he die, sir?'

'A horse stamped on his head. All I know about the human body I owe to this young gentleman. The hospital presented him to me when I attained my fiftieth year. An adornment, wouldn't you say, to this house?'

'Yes, sir.'

'Now you must go willingly to school – yes?'

'Yes, sir.'

'We shall converse again. Good day to you.'

'Do you think red hair would suit me?'

I looked up from the book I was reading.

'Did you hear what I asked you, You?'

'Yes, Mother.'

'Not that your opinion would sway me in one direction or the other. You just happen to be the only person here at the moment.'

'I can't imagine you with red hair – no.'

'Can't you? I can.'

'Dye it then.'

'I'll ask Dr Cottie before I do anything rash. He'll give the matter his consideration. He takes an interest, if you don't.'

I had guessed the nature of his 'interest' already. I would have been absurdly innocent if I hadn't: Mother's new found coquetry was sufficient evidence. Each time she announced that she was going up to the top floor to 'satisfy the doctor's requirements', an abrupt leer was added for emphasis. 'Even though he's retired, he still needs to practise his bedside manner.'

We couldn't eat our evening meal until the doctor's requirements had been satisfied. As Mother explained: 'If I eat before I go up to the doctor, I'll be coughing in his presence, and it isn't polite to cough when you're seeing to an elderly gentleman's needs.'

He was her hero for several months. The inevitable disillusionment set in gradually. 'That wonderful man on the top floor' became 'Him upstairs'; 'the elderly gentleman' changed into 'the old stoat'.

'Why do you call him a stoat, Mother?'

'Because I do.'

'It sounds daft to me.'

'You'll find out what I mean. One of these fine days.'

I knew what she meant even then, but wondered why she had chosen that particular animal. It was typical of Mother's obtuseness not to call Dr Cottie 'the old rabbit' – what it was about his sexual prowess that linked him in her mind with the stoat I never discovered. Perhaps he wore ermine in bed.

'Where he gets his energy from I simply don't know. For such a big man, he eats like a bird.'

It wasn't the vulture, certainly: steamed fish was to the doctor's taste, but not meat. He ate at regular hours and always sparingly. Breakfast was a mug of warm water and the yolk of a raw egg; lunch an uncooked Spanish onion with a few slices of cucumber surrounding it for decoration; in the early evening, when his requirements most needed satisfying, he drank a cup of tea ('Him and his broken Pekoe!') with lemon; while his last meal of the day consisted of a small piece of fish and a green vegetable washed down with two or three glasses of crusted port.

The lofty author of *With Stethoscope and Scalpel* overlooked these trifling domestic details: his book is distinguished by its scrupulous avoidance of anything remotely suggestive of human behaviour. No stoatish thoughts ever troubled the monumentally bland eunuch whose plodding progress it describes.

I remember lending Neville Drake a copy when we were lodging at Little Win's. 'Most books', he said, 'contain some cliches, but this one has them all.'

There have been Cotties in Plymouth since the time of the Norman conquest it begins, inaccurately. There is nothing in the files at Somerset House to substantiate the doctor's claim. *My esteemed ancestor, Lucas Cottie, sailed with 'famed Sir Francis' on* The Golden Hind. *It was my boyhood dream to emulate him and sail the seven seas like those swashbuckling salts of bygone days* ...

The doctor's birth certificate gives Leonard as his Christian name. His 'F', like the esteemed 'Lucas', is not recorded in fact.

The 'humble medic' who wrote of 'swashbuckling salts', who described the Astaires as 'those Terpsichorean enchanters', who 'threw caution to the winds' and 'ventured into the field of autobiography', was the owner of a superb collection of books. It still surprises me that a man who had read so widely—Homer, Dante, Jane Austen, Tolstoy, Flaubert—could have produced a work of such lifelessness.

While Mother and the doctor were occupied, I sat behind the huge roll-top desk in the library and surrendered myself to the authority of print. I jotted down in an exercise book the lines of poetry that most excited me:

> *Created sick, commanded to be sound ...*

and

> *Now more than ever seems it rich to die,*
> *To cease upon the midnight with no pain ...*

and

> *Fallings from us, vanishings ...*

and

> *He ruined mee, and I am re-begot*
> *Of absence, darknesse, death; things which are not ...*

I was happiest with negatives: the darker the vision, the lighter my heart.

> *Golden lads and girls all must,*
> *As chimney-sweepers, come to dust ...*

After our evening meal, with my ears closed to Mother's coughing, I studied until it was time to sleep. I had my dream to look forward to. I would walk in that eerily beautiful garden, now so unlike my grandmother's, and leave my shoes in the grass, and climb the tree when the German beckoned.

I was on a bus going over Westminster Bridge when I realized that my father would never return. The people near by had hands and eyes and were speaking to one another: as I looked at them and listened, the knowledge of his non-existence struck me. The pinkness of a stranger's tongue, glimpsed for a second, confirmed it. He was no longer among the living, as I was.

Then the smell of rain-sodden clothes reached me. I needed space to breathe in. I left the bus at the next stop. I tried to run, but my strangely heavy legs didn't take me far. I wanted not to think; I wanted the astonishment I felt at being astonished by something as obvious as Dad not having a pink tongue to go away. But it persisted. I thought of the rain muddying the earth above him, trickling down to his coffin, dripping on what was left of his unfeeling flesh.

'Are you mad, You? Are you? You're soaked to the skin. Do you want to catch your death?'

'I don't care.'

'You may not, you mad thing, but I do.'

'Do you?'

'I don't want the expense of it. I don't want people saying I neglected you, when I didn't, You. You're going to have a mustard bath this minute.'

I went to bed early that night. By now, astonishment had given way to shame. Why hadn't I thought of him in all those long months? The only time I'd remembered him was the evening I'd tried to impress Mother with my school reports, but even then it was Tommy I'd pictured first. I had feigned being dead that same evening to see if Mother would miss me.

I decided what to do: it would be real, and final; there would be no pretence about it. I waited until I heard Mother shut, and then lock, her bedroom door. (The stoat had wandered into the basement once.) I got up and walked on tiptoe to the kitchen. I opened the drawer in which she kept old pieces of brown paper and string — it was the latter I needed. I took the thickest I could find and went quietly up to the landing.

I made a noose at one end and put it round my neck. I tied the other end firmly to the banister, stood on the rail and threw myself off. The string broke; I landed on the hall carpet with a thump. I listened. The Elms was a burglar's paradise: no one stirred. I returned to my room with an aching back.

At breakfast the following morning, Mother said, 'I don't suppose you know why there's a length of string tied to the banister, do you, You?'

'Is there, Mother?'

57

'Yes, there is. Putting two and two together, I think that Him upstairs was practising his gymnastics in the middle of the night. He has some funny ways.'

The drawing showed a tall young man with lank hair and a sharp nose looking at a skull which he held like a mirror in his right hand. His thin black legs, with knees pointing inwards, made me think of a spider. A feather, slightly bent at the tip, stuck up from his hat. *Hamlet*—the caption read—*stands at Ophelia's graveside and recounts to his friend Horatio the tale of Yorick, the court jester*. There was no sign of the grave, though; and Horatio must have had exceptionally good hearing, for he was missing too.

I hadn't read far into the play before I knew that Sir Cecil Boxshall—the illustrator of this particular edition of Shakespeare in Dr Cottie's library—had failed to represent the prince's character. On page after page I was confronted by the Victorian academician's view of him: a pop-eyed Hamlet, with increasingly vulnerable knee-caps, and a tendency, as the drama progressed, to tear at his hair in a manner more refined then distraught.

I found another copy on the shelves, uncontaminated by Sir Cecil. I started the play again. I was on the last page, oblivious to everything else, when I became aware that Mother had entered the library.

'What's that you're poring over?'

'*Hamlet*.'

'Pull the other one, it's got bells on it. No boy of your age would be reading a stuffy old-fashioned thing like that the way you were when I came in. I've been stood here five minutes or more. Show your mother what you've been studying.'

I handed her the book.

'It says it's *Hamlet* sure enough. But boys of your age are crafty and don't I know it, You. I'll give it a shake. I bet you've got diagrams or even photos hidden inside it.'

A loose page fell to the floor. She pounced upon it.

'What did I say? Boys and their dirty minds! What did I say?'

She held it up to the light.

'It looks like words. And I have a fair idea what type of words they are, too. I'll get my glasses to this, I will. Downstairs with you, come on.'

I did as Gertrude told me.

'Now I'll find out what you're poring over when you say you're doing your parlee-vous.' She took her spectacles out of their case. She sniffed the page and put it on the kitchen table. 'Mm,' she said, 'Mm. Well, yes. Mm. You wouldn't catch me reading stuff like this.'

'He doesn't join the Foreign Legion.'

'Who doesn't?'

'Hamlet.'

'There wasn't such a thing when Shakespeare was about. Even I know that, and I haven't had your education. You tell me you're little Mr Clever Dick when it comes to history, and then you make a remark like that.'

She tried to read it upside down. Perhaps she suspected a code.

'I'll catch you one of these fine days.'

'You won't, Mother.'

'I will.'

'I never look at diagrams.'

'I should hope not. All those details. Well, sitting here keeping track of your dirty mind isn't getting his fish cooked or our stew ready. Put the plates out, You.'

'Yes, Mother.'

'Why are you sounding sarcastic?'

'Am I, Mother?'

'Don't call me Mother in that tone. You bring them into the world and all you get for thanks is insults.'

'Thank you for bringing me into the world, Mother.'

She stared at me in disbelief. She cleared her throat – if there was a rumble below, I didn't hear it. She spoke in a surprisingly tired voice: 'You can take his fish up tonight. I've done enough today to keep him happy.'

I carried the plate of haddock and cabbage up to Claudius. I knocked at his door.

'No need for ceremony, Nelly.'

'It's me,' I said. 'Sir.'

'One moment. One moment.'

Several minutes later he told me to enter.

'Aha. Food.'

'I'm afraid it's got a bit cold, sir. I had to wait so long outside.'

'My apologies for delaying you. Will you drink a glass of crusted port with me?'

'I—'

'Not accustomed—are you—to alcohol?'

'I've drunk beer.'

'That was manly of you.' He did a bad impersonation of Cockney: 'Not me potion at all.' He smiled wanly. 'I'll pour you a small measure.'

'Where shall I put your meal, sir?'

'On the bed, if you would be so kind.'

They've just been honeying here, I said to myself.

'Don't gulp it. Savour it. Let it linger on your palate.'

I took the poisoned cup from him.

'To an industrious young man.'

I sipped the port while he ate.

'You will forgive me, I trust, being thus attired?'

He was wearing a gold dressing-gown.

'Yes, sir.'

'Most nutritious. You are watching me rather closely.'

'Am I, sir?'

'But learning too, I hope. I am a slow eater—that you will have observed. I have perfect digestion. The small amount of food I take in each day is made to do its work. My wheels, so to speak, run smoothly. They do not grind to a halt. They are well-oiled.'

'Are they, sir?'

'They are. Your mother—does she—gives you cabbage to eat?'

'Yes, sir. Lots of it.'

'Sensible woman. It puts—to quote the old saw—lead in your pencil.'

'Lead in my pencil?'

'Precisely. Lead in your pencil.'

'I don't understand, sir.'

'How old are you?'

'Nearly fourteen.'

'You should understand by that age. Lead, er, is a euphemism. You have heard the word "euphemism"?'

'Yes, sir.'

'Well, er, lead signifies one's—one's substance. You know where your substance comes from?'

'No, sir.'

'You surprise me. On the verge of fourteen, and unaware! Well, er, it comes—your substance, that is—from your pencil. Pencil, as you have probably guessed, is a euphemism too.'

'Is it, sir?'

'It is.'

'What for, sir?'

'Well, er—which part of your body would you say most resembles a pencil?'

I pretended to think deeply: my brow became suitably furrowed. I looked at the doctor and smiled. He smiled back.

'Aha!'

'My index finger, of course, sir.'

'Well, er, yes. One could compare one's digits to a pencil; yes, one could. The particular pencil to which I am referring is located somewhat lower on the person.'

'Toes, sir?'

'No. Not toes. No, not toes at all. Which, er, part of your body is, er, capable—and sometimes without manual assistance—of, well, growth?'

'Growth, sir?'

'Yes, growth. It goes up, and then it comes down.'

'I can't imagine, sir.'

'Imagination is unnecessary in this case. It is a simple matter of seeing what is, er, in front of you. In the morning, when you awaken, nothing happens—does it—to your, er, hosepipe?'

'Hosepipe?'

'Never at a tilt, is it? Never rigid?'

'My hosepipe?'

'Your waterworks, lad, your—'

'My cock, sir?'

'Precisely. The word "cock" is also a euphemism, and not—to my mind—either an exact or, indeed, a salutary one. I do not—it is my whim, I admit—approve of foul language.'

'That's very funny, sir.'

'Funny? What is?'

'Your joke, sir.'

'Joke?'

'Your use of words. "Cock", sir—if you'll excuse me—and "foul language".'

'Oh, yes. Quite unintended. A slip of the tongue.'

'So my substance comes—does it—from my ... ?'

'You hesitate.'

'You don't approve, sir, of the word.'

'Ah, yes. Your penis. That is the *mot juste*.'

'Thank you, sir.'

'You are—in one department at least—a late starter. You will discover, in time, that the cabbage will prove to be beneficial. Do not be alarmed when it happens.'

'Thank you, sir. Have you finished your meal, sir?'

'Not quite. My progress has been impeded by our most interesting conversation.' He cleaned the plate. ' "Yum, yum", as you no doubt say in schoolboy fashion after a satisfactory repast. "Yum, yum." '

'I'll tell Mother you enjoyed it, sir.'

'I should be obliged.'

Gertrude was glowering when I returned to the kitchen.

'Where have you been, You?'

'Upstairs, Mother, with the doctor.'

'I know he's a fussy eater, but he doesn't usually take as long as this.'

'He was talking to me.'

'I can believe it. He loves the sound of his own voice, does that man. Most men do.'

'Dad didn't.'

'We won't discuss him.'

'Why not?'

'Y's the twenty-fifth letter of the alphabet, and a knot is something you tie.'

'Dad didn't love the sound of his own voice. He hardly ever spoke.'

'Sit down and eat your stew.'

'Are you going to marry Dr Cottie?'

'Are you going to eat your food?'

'I'm not hungry.'

'I'll only warm it up again tomorrow, if you don't.'

'I shan't be hungry then either.'

'No, I'm not going to marry him.'

'I thought you were.'

'You thought! What gave you that idea?'

'He calls you Nelly.'

'It's my name.'

'Dad never called you Nelly.'

'What did he say to you up there?'

'Aha!'

'That old snob wouldn't marry me in a month of Sundays. He wants a skivvy, he does; someone to jump at his every command. Would he be seen dead in the street with me? No, he wouldn't.'

'So you aren't going to marry him?'

'I wish I'd been a fly on the wall when you were up there with him. He didn't show you diagrams, did he?'

'No, Mother.'

'I should hope not.'

'Did you ever want to marry him?'

'Marry, marry, marry — I'm fed up with you saying that.'

'You haven't answered me.'

'I'll answer you with the back of my hand if you don't watch your step.'

'Mrs F. Leonard Cottie.'

'Catch me making a fool of myself twice in one lifetime.'

'Did you love Dad?'

'Love!'

'Did you?'

'You're too young to know about such things. Love, I ask you. Love!'

'Like Sir Eustace felt for Imelda?'

'Who are they with their daft names?'

'Can't you tell me you loved him? Can't you honestly tell me?'

'I thought your father would have done better for himself than he did. He was Smart by name, he was, but not by nature. Always blaming his lack of will-power on that Blighty wound.'

'You said it killed him.'

'I don't remember saying that.'

'I do.'

'Well, it probably did have something to do with him passing on when he did, but not so much as he'd have people believe—'

'He's dead, Mother.'

'Are your screws loose, You? If he was alive, we wouldn't be here in the old stoat's servants' quarters, would we?'

'Oh, I give up.'

'I should hope so. Your questions have worn me to a frazzle, they have. I'm all unsettled.'

I wanted to do something dramatic with the stew, but decided against it. I was suddenly ravenous. I sat down and ate.

Reading *Hamlet,* I was reminded of one of Granny Smart's books— *The Fatal Cup of Cocoa.* A stockbroker's wife in Purley had fallen madly in love with a sinister Polish chemist who had bought the house next door. Each day, as soon as the stockbroker left for the City, the Pole sneaked in through the conservatory and proceeded to bend the woman to his will. Held captive by his charm, and swayed by a passion that changed her from a contented housewife into a monster of depravity, she gave herself body and soul to the immigrant with the ice-cold eyes. On his instructions, she added arsenic to her dogged husband's bedtime drink. The evil pair would have got away with their dreadful deed had not a neighbour been seriously disturbed by the shocking sounds of their love-making a mere hour after the funeral. Mrs Tillit, whose evidence sent the foreign fiend to the gallows, had invited some ladies in for tea that afternoon: imagine their surprise when the air was suddenly filled with noises more appropriate to the jungle than a respectable English suburb. No one had had the stomach for walnut cake.

From Claudius in the orchard, with his vial of 'cursed hebona', my mind went to the unforgettably named Ainslie Gritter's account of the Purley stockbroker's dying moments: the victim's face, he wrote, 'turned as green as a Bramley apple'. Then I remembered my father's complexion the night before his death. Had Mother, influenced by F. Leonard Cottie, poisoned him?

'You've been giving me strange looks lately, you have, You.'

'Have I, Mother?'

'Yes, you have, and you can just stop it. Staring's rude, as I thought I'd taught you.'

No, it was too far-fetched; it was impossible to picture her slipping poison into Dad's tea. She didn't look like a monster of depravity as she stood at the sink peeling potatoes. She belonged in the ordinary world, where murders didn't happen. Her hair wasn't standing on end; her eye-balls weren't rolling.

'Have you got nothing better to do than to sit there watching me work? Are you so clever already that you don't have to study any more, You?'

'Oh no, Mother.'

'A modest little flower for once in his life. Well, pick up a book and occupy yourself; the hours you waste never return again, and that's a truth. One of these fine days you'll live to regret your idleness.'

'I was wondering –'

'Wondering won't sweep the parlour clean or pin the baby back together.'

'What?'

'He invented steam.'

'What did you mean when you mentioned the baby, Mother?'

'Mother meant that wondering doesn't change a baby's nappy, that's what Mother meant, You.'

'Which baby?'

' "Which baby?" he asks. Any baby. It's a saying. And a true one.'

'I see.'

'I should hope so. Education!'

'What I was wondering was –'

'You're still in the land of dreams, are you?'

'No. I was – I won't say wondering –'

'A change is as good as a rest—'

'I was *thinking*: could it be that Dad didn't die of pneumonia?'

'What put that thought in your head?'

'I don't know.'

'I should hope not.'

'It seemed wrong—his going quickly like that. And in such hot weather.'

'Hot or cold, wet or fine, when you have to go, you go.'

'Gran said—'

'I might have known that old tramp would have put her spoke in somewhere.'

'She said it was strange, dying of pneumonia in the summer—'

'Oh, she's an expert, is she? A doctor, is she? You could go to her and get treated, could you? You never heed a word I say, which is something I've noticed about you, but you listen to her as if she was giving out the gospel. It's unnatural for a boy to be so morbid, and it's all her fault. You concern yourself with the here and now, You, and leave the dead to their rest.'

'Yes, Mother.'

'One of these fine days, you'll say yes to me and mean it.'

'But I do now.'

'No, you don't. You've become sly. You're not the nice, honest boy you were. You've changed.'

'When was I nice and honest, Mother?'

'Your school cap's tight enough on your head as it is, without praise from me to make it tighter. I don't know what's got into you lately. Sometimes I think that skeleton upstairs has more life in him.'

'Your mother has not abandoned you.'

The doctor, wearing a pinafore, was in the kitchen.

'She has left you in my incapable hands for a few days. She has been called to northern parts. A parent—she did not specify which—is ailing.'

'Her mother.'

'Aha.'

'She's in a bin.'

'A bin?'

'A lunatic asylum.'

'Oh? An inmate, is she? Mind unhinged?'

'Yes, sir.'

'A delicate mechanism, so very delicate. Disturb the balance, and chaos ensues. I have—have I not?—borne witness to that chaos.'

'Have you, sir?'

'I have.'

He slapped his face with a dish-cloth and laughed.

'Whoa there, F. Leonard. Whoa! Bring yourself to heel!'

'Sir?'

He continued to address himself: 'Talking of such matters with a mere stripling! "In youth is pleasure", remember. The dark comes soon enough.'

'Does it, sir?'

'It does. Let us turn our attention to life's more pleasurable aspects. Food, for example. You have not, I trust, spoiled your appetite by consuming tuck?'

'No, sir.'

'You are a most untypical schoolboy. Restraining hands had to be put on me whenever I found myself in the vicinity of that tiny shop—aha, I see it now—in which the ever-smiling Miss Prentice sold cream buns of a size to satisfy Gargantua. Yes, indeed—re-straining hands.'

'You don't eat very much now, sir.'

'No, I do not.'

'Why don't you?'

'A garden full of weeds does not delight the eye.'

'Sir?'

'The body, similarly, should be kept in trim condition. Fat is as unsightly as ragwort. I am a large man; persons of limited growth would describe me as a *very* large man, but I do not—no, no, I definitely do not—suffer from an excess of weight on my still energetic limbs. Butt me.'

'Butt you, sir?'

'Precisely. Butt me. You are a ferocious bull, and I am the matador, swirling his elegant cape. My stomach is, at this moment, exciting your wrath. Your horns are aimed in its direction. Butt it.'

I lowered my head and ran towards him.

'Timid, timid bull! Charge! Charge!'

My head met his stomach. He swayed slightly. I lost my balance and fell to the floor.

'Hard, wasn't it?'

'Yes, sir.'

'Firm as a rock?'

'Yes, sir.'

I stood up.

'Let us now—shall we?—oil our wheels.'

'Thank you, sir.'

He sang as he drained the greens:

> ' "Fascinating Rhythm,
>   You've got me on the go!
>   Fascinating Rhythm,
>   I'm all a-quiver ... " '

He brought the plates to the table.

'Bon appetit!'

'And you, sir.'

'Cod.'

'Delicious, sir.'

'A favourite fish—if my memory serves me right—in northern parts.'

'Is it, sir?'

'In the far north, certainly.'

The cod was dry and tasteless. I tried to eat it quickly, but the doctor checked me:

'Savour it, boy, savour it. It won't be of benefit if it's gulped down.'

'Yes, sir.'

'Your stool—is it—is regular?'

'I can't see a stool. I'm sitting on a chair.'

'You misunderstand me. Your bowels—do they—open at the same time each day?'

'No, sir. Sometimes in the morning; sometimes at night.'

'Bad. You must regulate them. Don't allow them to be capricious. Tell them, and tell them firmly, when to discharge their load. Eight o'clock, say, or nine, or even seven: early or late; the hour is unimportant. Once you have decided, allow no variation. Health, health abounding, will be the result.'

'I'll try to be regular, sir.'

'You will succeed, I am sure.'

I drank a glass of crusted port with the doctor and then we washed the dishes.

'A stroll in the evening air — would it — would be acceptable?'

'I have to read about George Fox —'

'Let him wait. It is balmy outside. You can peruse the Quaker's perorations on our return. Remember this: too much close reading when young ensures a dowager's hump in middle age. Think of the future, and exercise.'

Apart from telling me to keep my head up and my shoulders back, the doctor said nothing until we reached Kensington Gardens.

'Aha, the flowers of spring are blooming already.'

'Yes, sir.'

'Not exactly "A host of golden daffodils", but a sufficient number to delight the eye.'

The doctor stopped occasionally to sniff the flowers, most of which had no scent. He was drawing himself up from a hyacinth when he suddenly exclaimed 'Good God, I don't believe it!'

'Sir?'

'Follow my eyes!'

His demented stare made me think of the Ancient Mariner.

'Look at that man. Look at him closely.'

A purple-faced tramp had provoked Dr Cottie's interest.

'Does anything strike you?'

'His nose needs blowing.'

'Yes, yes — what else?'

'He's feeding the pigeons.'

'That does not make him interesting. Study his features.'

'His skin's a funny colour.'

'Aha! A good deduction, Watson. Let's see if you reach the

69

same conclusion as your friend Holmes. Look again.'

'His jaw—'

'Yes? Yes?'

'There's something wrong with it.'

'Phosphonecrosis.'

'What's that, sir?'

'A man with your training, my dear Watson, should know what that is.' A gurgle escaped from him. 'That poor wretch has inhaled phosphorus. In a factory, no doubt, where matches were made. It is a rare disease. I have encountered it only once before in my long career. And now, him—some twenty years after.'

He went over to the tramp and put out his hand.

'Shake it.'

'Why should I do a thing like that?'

'You are a survivor. I wish to pay my respects.'

'I don't want them.'

'You have weathered life bravely.'

'Who said so?'

'I say so. Your modesty does you proud. Since you refuse—with a dignity that greatly impresses me—to accept my hand-shake, will you allow me instead to honour an unsung hero?'

The doctor clicked his heels and saluted the tramp. The man, who had looked at him up to this point with suspicion, now smiled broadly, revealing immaculate dentures.

'I don't see why you shouldn't. All things considered.'

They shook hands.

'I don't suppose—Oh no, I couldn't ask it of a gentleman—'

'What couldn't you ask?'

'The price of a cup of tea?'

'Put on your best bib and tucker.' The doctor gave the tramp a five pound note. 'Have it at the Ritz.'

Mother returned.

'Did Him upstairs cook your dinners?'

'Yes.'

'Eatable, were they?'

'Yes. Very.'

'I bet. I bet they were!'

'The one I cooked was the best.'

'It was, was it? I can see you'll be short of breath when you grow up.'

'What?'

'He invented steam.'

'Why will I be short of breath?'

'Because you blow your own trumpet too much.'

I didn't tell her that I wanted to die. I think I shrugged.

'Look at the dust!'

I looked. There was none to be seen.

'It's as if I'd been away for a year!'

'Yes.'

'I didn't ask for your opinion on the subject.' An imaginary cobweb received vicious treatment from the handle of Mother's broom. 'Well, I shan't have to go up there any more. That's one comfort, I suppose.'

'Up where, Mother?'

'Up North, among those heathens. They're not the type of people I care to mix with, that lot aren't. They haven't a "Thank you" in them — you just try giving them something if you don't believe me, You. From Doncaster onwards, they're all the same.'

'Is she dead then?'

'What?'

'He invented steam, Mother.'

'Don't you give me lip, You.'

'Is she dead?'

'If it's my Mam you're talking about —'

'Who else?'

'Did *he* tell you?'

'Dad? Yes.'

'He'd no right. It was wrong of him. He'd no right. He didn't tell you, did he, where she lived?'

'Yes.'

'Trust him. Well, she's gone now. It was a merciful release, and that's a truth. I've nothing more to say about it.'

She pointed at the ceiling and asked if a certain person had been showing me any diagrams.

'No.'

'I should hope not.'

'My Mam.' Perhaps, when she spoke to strangers, I was 'my boy' or 'my son' or—strangest sounding of all—'my Peter'. I never heard from them; I never found out.

'What was Mrs Dixon like, Mother?'

'He told you her name as well, did he? I'm surprised he didn't tell you what she was wearing when he met her.'

'Was she gentle?'

'That's a daft question for a boy to ask.'

'Was she?'

'You sound as if you want to know.'

'I do.'

'She was and she wasn't.'

She sniffed the evening paper before opening it.

'Let her be.'

Safe behind the *Star*, she complained of the state of the world—the people in it had little to be proud of. Further discussion of Mrs Dixon's misery was abandoned in favour of larger issues: 'If I ever met Ernest Bevin in the street—which God forbid—I'd call him a fool to his face, I would. A few sharp words from a sensible person would soon buck his ideas up.'

The Elms was Elsinore that summer. The insubstantial ghost of my father had begun to haunt me.

'Have you seen how pale you are, You? Wandering about the house with that moony expression on your face—it's not natural. You should be out in the sunshine.'

I tried, as I wandered through rooms and along passages, to reassemble the bits and pieces that had once been Gerald Smart. A hero did not emerge. It grieved me to discover that you could look upon his like wherever you turned, whatever the time of day: he'd made no mark; his only talent was for vanishing.

Even so, I missed his unimpressive presence. I resented the fact that his inadequacy could no longer be challenged. I wanted to know why, losing Alice, he had chosen Ellen. Had she been beautiful then, and gentle? Had he found words to convey what he felt for her? Had she offered her wounded soldier peace?

'I've called you three times for your breakfast, You.'

'Yes, Mother.'

'Don't "Mother" me in that tone. Just put some life in your limbs.'

She pulled back the sheet. I was naked.

'What have you got pyjamas for? Ornaments?'

'I felt too hot to wear them last night.'

'Heat or no heat, I want you to grow up respectable.' She watched me as I left the bed, my hands covering a piss erection. 'That hasn't grown much since I last caught sight of it.'

'What hasn't?'

'Never you mind.'

When I went into the kitchen she was ironing the doctor's *Times*.

'There's been a murder.'

'Murder?'

'That's what I said. Who would have believed it? I'd have thought Kensington was the last place on earth it could happen in.'

'Here?'

'Not on these premises, God spare us, no. In the mews, round the back. I'd have expected it where we used to live – south of the river, anything can happen – but not in a royal borough.'

'Who was it?'

'You're lively for a change today. Since you're so anxious to know, it was a titled gentleman.'

'How was he murdered?'

'You *are* morbid, and that's a truth. Someone croaks, and your eyes light up. He was strangled.'

'Who by?'

'I wasn't a fly on the wall, was I? The police have no idea, so why should I have? Your food's not for staring at – it's for eating, You. Looking at a cold fried egg turns my stomach, so get it inside you before I have a fit.'

'Yes, Mother.'

'Haven't you got any friends at that school?'

'One or two.'

'Why don't you meet them in the holidays?'

'They've gone away.'

'If the old stoat can bear to let me have a day off, I might take you to the seaside.'

'Thank you.'

'Are you thinking about him again?'

'Who?'

'Your father.'

'Yes.'

'I thought so. You shouldn't.'

'Shouldn't?'

'Yes. You pay your respects to the living. The dead can't be helped.'

The doctor rang for service.

'I wish Him upstairs had a little less life in his body, I can tell you. I wish there was something – a pill or a tablet – I could slip into his glass of water.'

'What for, Mother?'

'Just to quieten him down. He ought to be in a bath chair, the age he is.'

'You never gave Dad a pill, did you?'

'He needed one to wake him up, your father did. I may have given him a few things to think about, You, but I never gave him a pill, no.'

She shouted from the stairs: 'I gave him plenty of poultices, though. For his war wound.'

It wasn't possible, I told myself. Why, she, even she, wasn't capable of murder. I was a schoolboy, not a prince. My father had been a clerk, not a king. It wasn't possible. Kings didn't complain that their vegetables had been 'boiled to buggery'; they didn't sneak out of the palace for a plate of jellied eels as soon as the banquet was over. No, it just wasn't possible.

'Is it still going on?' Mother's voice came from the broom cupboard. 'I can scarcely breathe in here.'

'It won't be through for a long time yet.'

'I always think the lightning's aimed at me.'

As the storm progressed, I assured myself that the days of lethargy were over. From now on, not a moment would be wasted. I drew blood from my arm with Gerald Smart's penknife. I was alive. The air cooled, and I became warm.

'Has it finished, You?'

'No. No!'

'You don't have to shout. The thunder's deafening enough, without you adding to it.'

That hunched-up coward under the stairs would be proud of me yet.

'If the old stoat's bell rings, you'll have to go up and tell him I'm feeling poorly. Don't you dare let him know where I am. You hear me?'

'Yes.'

'You won't keep me in here out of spite, will you, once it's ended?'

'Why should I?'

'There's those who would, and that's a truth.'

'I'm not one of them, Mother.'

'I should hope not.'

She came out of the cupboard on all fours.

'You could help me to my feet, You.'

I pulled her up by the shoulders. She shook invisible dust from her frock and said, 'Who's got a gleam in his eye, then?'

'Me?'

'I can't see anyone else. You look as mad as Moses when he saw the tablets. I swear you're not natural – you're either high in the clouds, or deep in the dumps. Why you can't stay flat on the earth, I'll never understand.'

I was about to write a masterpiece; that was why.

'How did you cut yourself?'

'I'm not sure.'

'I'm sure you're not.'

Its title had come to me. *The Night Before Battle*.

'Trust you to leave it to bleed. I suppose I'd better find a plaster for it. I don't want you going down with gangrene.'

The following morning I went to a stationer's in the City and bought a fat leather-bound ledger. It looked imposing enough to contain the great work of literature I was anxious to get started on. Clutching it to my chest, I hurried back to The Elms.

I set Sebastian rattling and entered the library. Surrounded by classics, I felt confident of creating another. Nothing less would do. I sat behind the doctor's desk, sharpened a pencil, opened the ledger and printed in large letters on the first page:

THE

NIGHT

BEFORE

BATTLE

BY

PETER SMART

Which night? What battle? I didn't know, as yet. All I was certain of was that the holidays were nearly at an end: I had just two weeks and a day in which to produce the play or novel that would secure me a place among the immortals. It was a challenge I had to rise to. With the white heat of inspiration consuming me, I reasoned, I would have time and to spare.

My writing hand committed the words 'Act One' to paper, and the epic drama was under way. A few minutes later, the hero – a very old, very wise man with a very long beard – emerged from his mountain cave and greeted the sun. Philo was still addressing Phoebus (a remarkably patient and considerate listener) when Mother walked in and broke my flow.

'I should have known you'd be in the Temple of Wisdom, as Him upstairs calls this place. He'd soon give it a different name if he had to take a duster to it. Here's my grocery list, You – get down to the shop and make yourself useful.'

'I'm busy.'

'At what?'

'Writing.'

'The world's waited centuries to hear from you, so I think it can afford to wait a bit longer. If you want food in your belly tonight, you'll do as I ask.'

'Must I? This minute?'

'Yes, you must. Straight away.'

Food! What did I want with food? I told Mother that Handel, interrupted by his housekeeper during the composition of the *Messiah,* refused the broth she offered him by observing that it wasn't food for the body he needed, it was food for the soul.

'There's a garret above the doctor's bedroom if you require somewhere to starve.'

Philo had run out of thoughts when I got back with the groceries. I introduced a monk into the action (who else would bother to visit an old man on a mountain?), but after an exchange of pleasantries ('Another hot day awaits us, Elder'; 'Ay, the good sun will warm me') Father Anselm's conversational gifts proved to be less than adequate:

PHILO. Is it true that, down below, a battle rages, Father?
ANSELM. Yes.

I put in some atmosphere: a bird sang; crickets chirped. A goat came on and drank at a stream. Philo commented on the beauty of God's creatures, and the monk added an appreciative 'Yes'.

ANSELM (*Appreciatively*). Yes.

Before I went down to the kitchen that evening, I covered my precious ledger in brown paper. I wrote the title on the front. On the back, I quoted extensively from Jean Cocteau's review in *Le Figaro Litteraire*: ' "La Ville avant la Bataille" est une œuvre de génie, gigantesque et à la même fois profonde ... ' and so on.

The next day, after much agonizing, I scrapped what I'd written and began work on a novel. Thomas Mann thought well of it. He gave his opinion in English: 'This rich narrative has made a colossal impression on me. The author has plunged into the very deep well of the past and brought up a creation of genius ... '

With only a week to go before school began I had reached the end of the third paragraph and awarded myself the Nobel Prize. Wanting words, I filled the pages with drawings – of the kind Mother called 'diagrams'. The longer I sat waiting for inspiration, the more I was prone to stoatish imaginings. Two things excited me: the down on my friend Hudson's legs, and Pam Bridle's nipples. Pam was a pig-breeder's daughter whose bust had once been the talk of the village.

'They grow bigger with every day that passes. Just look at them, our Peter. She'll be needing a cart to carry them in by the time she's fifteen. I swear her father feeds her on swill.'

'She showed them to me, Gran.'

'Did she now, the trollop!'

'She let me touch them. She charged me a penny.'

'She'll end up cold meat at some man's hands, as sure as God made little apples. You'd best stay away from her, my lad.'

Poor Pam had died, at no man's hands, of natural causes, young. Closing my eyes, I saw her alive again, under the holm-oak behind the church, offering her titties to the choir.

'Would Master Will Shakespoke care to come down for his evening repast? Or do I have to come up there and fetch him, You?'

I turned Pam's breasts into funny faces and closed the ledger.

'Irish stew. It'll build you up for the winter. Hay fever, is it, You?'

'What?'

We said 'He invented steam' in unison.

'I don't know what writing tripe in that big book is doing to you, but you seem to be getting through more handkerchiefs than usual. I thought you might have hay fever, even though I haven't heard you sneeze.'

'Haven't you, Mother?'

'No, I have not!' she shouted.

Decorating my masterpiece the next day, I made sure that Mother heard.

She put her head round the library door, grimaced, and said, 'Bless you.'

I got into the habit of interviewing myself as I walked from Lambeth to Kensington.

Mr Smart—I believe you have just completed your twentieth book. What is it about?

The decline of a civilization.

What are you writing now?
A major tragedy …
The interviews took a slightly different course after I was chosen to play Lady Macbeth:
Sir Peter — I must congratulate you on your amazing Oedipus.
Thank you.
What are you rehearsing at this moment?
Lear …
'Mother, can you guess what's happened to me?'
'I shudder to think.'
'I'm going to be Lady Macbeth.'
'Whatever for?'
'I'm going to act. At school.'
'I didn't figure you'd be doing it in the street. Why aren't you playing His Lordship?'
'Mr Campbell doesn't want me to.'
'And I'd like to know why. It isn't natural, a boy being asked to cavort—'
'Cavort?'
'Cavort. I do know a word or two, You; my head's not made of clay, although there are those who'd argue to the contrary.'
'Boys played women at the Globe.' She stared at me. 'Four hundred years ago.'
'That was then. This is now.'
'Yes, Mother.'

I willed my hands to stop shaking. I clutched Macbeth's letter and walked on.

Someone started to clap. It was Dr Cottie, seated in the centre of the front row. Someone's mother told him to shut up in a loud voice.

My throat was dry, my head empty, my body paralysed. I opened my mouth and by some miracle the right words came out. From that moment, Peter Smart ceased to exist; only the Lady lived.

I rose from the dead when the audience applauded me. I

curtsied. A bright light shone on me. Released from my long absorption, I glowed.

'A red wig, he said. And a green dress. You didn't wear jewels as well, did you, You?'

'A necklace.'

'Earrings?'

'No.'

'I should hope not.'

'I wore a bracelet too.'

'Round your ankle?'

'No, Mother.'

'I might come along and watch it tomorrow, if I can spare the time. Looking after a house this size makes demands on a person. It was typical of Him upstairs not to suffer my presence at his side tonight. "You must stay here and keep the burglars at bay" —that's what he said when I mentioned that I wouldn't mind going with him to see my own son acting on the stage. He's an old snob, and that's a truth.'

'You *must* come and see me.'

'No "must" about it.'

'It would make me happy if you did.'

'I dare say it would. I've more to do with my life than seeing that you keep a smile on your face—you just remember. Go to bed.'

Mother's harsh laugh greeted me at breakfast.

'Who's the honoured one, then?'

She handed me a parcel.

'The gentleman on the top floor asked me to give it to you. With his compliments—for what they're worth.'

She laughed again as I tore the wrapping.

'You *are* in a state of excitement, aren't you, You? Calm yourself. It's only his life story. "With Whichway and Whatnot", or whatever he calls it.'

The doctor had written on the fly-leaf: 'To a talented young Thespian, who will one day add Lustre to the English Stage. From a humble "Fan". F. Leonard Cottie.'

'I call it piffle.'

'Have you read it?'

'I stuck my nose in it a couple of times. Very medical, they were, the bits I glanced at. Lots of nasty words. You needn't look so pleased with yourself – he made me a present of it, too. Apart from nightmares, it's about the only thing he *has* given me.'

Mother came to the performance that evening. I heard her tell Mr Campbell how proud of me she was. 'He's been hiding his light under a bushel, just like his poor father did.'

On the way back to The Elms, I asked her what she thought of my acting.

'I'd take a man's part next time if I were you.'

We were silent for the rest of the journey. Her shoes 'for special occasions' squeaked and squeaked and squeaked. She smiled and smiled and smiled until her agony was over.

Then Granny died.

Mother put on her glasses, took the telegram out of its envelope and sniffed it.

'This might interest you. It doesn't me.'

'MA PASSED OVER SUNDAY FUNERAL FRIDAY HILDA MOSFORD', I read.

'She gives herself his name even though he never took her to the altar.'

'When are we going, Mother?'

'When are *you* going? you mean. You can go – for the sake of appearances – but you won't catch me putting my best black on for her. I may have failings, but at least I'm honest. Hers is one funeral I wouldn't be seen dead at.'

I travelled to Portsmouth with the doctor's memoirs for company. He was born; he had a contented childhood; he 'attended a famed academy'. He abandoned a naval career and decided to serve as a 'humble medic' after hearing Sir Royston Hammond ('of Fond Memory') lecture on disorders of the cranium. He prospered: 'I attained my thirtieth year and the title of Doctor.' In the fourth chapter – 'My First Hernia' – he 'craved the reader's indulgence for a little digression'. What, I wondered, were 'Malgaigne's bulgings'? What was a 'hernioplasty'? The doctor didn't say. Mist descended. I persevered. What was a 'hepatocele'? How did it differ from a 'scrotocele'? The mist thickened. If you suffered from 'Dietl's crises', did they give you 'Eisenmenger's complex'? What, or where, was the 'sphincter of Oddi'?

I sweltered in the tropics; I froze in the Arctic; I was home.

'I want to see her, Aunt Hilda.'

'I don't think you should, Peter. You're still a boy, for all the grown-up airs you've got.'

'I used to help her when she went visiting – don't you remember?'

I had my way. I saw her. She had been washed and dressed: her shroud was cleaner than anything she had worn in life. I kissed her: she smelled of beer and snuff, not soap. I closed the coffin lid.

The saintly creature Reverend Chartle described sounded nothing like my brown grandmother. His sermon seemed longer than the doctor's digression. There were yawns. We sang 'Immortal, Invisible': Aunt Hilda deafeningly, tunelessly. Her hands were clasped firmly together. They became fish again when we stood at the graveside.

'I've only myself to tidy for now.'

Frank Burgess, whom Granny had called 'Edna' because of his habit of dressing up in his wife's clothes and singing rude songs every Saturday night, laid on a farewell spread in The Wheatsheaf. We drank stout, ate cold pork and ham, and exchanged memories.

'I bet you don't remember, Pete, that Jerry soldier in your Granny's garden.'

'I do, Mrs Long.'

'Why, you were only a tiddler at the time. You ought to stay down here, my lad, rather than go back to that there London place – there's more goes on here, I swear, than ever does in that dirty great dump. Since you were here all that while ago, we've had enough things happening to fill a book. Did you hear tell of Arthur Simmons?'

'The postman?'

'If he'd bought some French letters, there'd have been no delivery,' said Frank Burgess. Everyone laughed.

'Don't you dare say any more, Minnie Long.'

'Hush, Hilda, he's of an age now. Look at him, he's bursting to hear. He knows what the good God gave him that bit of extra flesh for. He's well aware that it's not for stirring his tea with.'

'What did he do?'

'Not *what*, son — *who*', said Frank Burgess. Everyone laughed again.

'He put a bun in his daughter's oven. Only a week after he'd put one in his wife's. He told us all that a Yank had got at her in Southampton, but we know better.'

'How?'

'She told us.'

'His daughter?'

'Boasts about it, she does. She says she loves her Dad — he's the only man in her life. You can't help but pity her. She's daft, Pete. She's touched.'

I was drunk when I boarded the bus for Portsmouth.

'I'm glad your mother didn't come, Peter.'

'So am I.'

'She would have cast a shadow. I wanted Ma to be sent off happy.'

'She was.'

I recollect, with shame, what I said to Aunt Hilda as we parted. 'Keep the house tidy for me.' I never went back.

'Happy birthday.'

'Thank you, Mother.'

'I've bought you a white shirt. Why people have to be given presents just because it's the anniversary of the day they were born, I can't understand. But if they *have* to receive something, it might as well be useful.'

'Yes, Mother. Thank you.'

'You can wear it today with your suit.'

'Why? It's too hot to — '

'Because the doctor is taking you out, that's why. You know perfectly well that he always dresses like a tailor's dummy, and I don't want you showing me up.' She added, mysteriously: 'The

83

'old fool says he can't explain things on the premises; he'd rather do it his way, outside.'

'Explain?'

'Yes. It's a man's task, not a woman's. I can just picture your father doing it, at the rate of one word per hour.' She shrieked: 'What little he knew!'

Mother inspected me when I had bathed and dressed.

'You look as presentable as you ever will, You. I wish your hair was a shade darker, but there's nothing I can do about it now. The lord and master of The Elms is waiting for you in the hall.'

The doctor shook my hand. 'You have attained your sixteenth year?'

'Yes, sir.'

'The time has come – has it not? – for you to taste the fruit. Let us go. No, no, young man – after you.'

He opened the door for me. We went down to the street.

'Which route shall we take? Shall we stroll in an easterly direction?'

We set off.

'Your brain, F. Leonard, your brain. Employ it! Westward ho, young man. Through the park.'

He raised his hat to Mother, who was staring out of the library window, as we passed the cul-de-sac. I saw her put a finger to the side of her head and turn it. Someone, she was indicating, had a screw loose.

The first of our many walks that day ended at Marble Arch, where 'we availed ourselves of underground transportation'.

The doctor handed me a note: 'Study the woman seated opposite.'

I looked at her – she was fat; her sandalled feet were dirty; she had hairs sprouting from her chin.

The doctor gave me his pen. 'She has a beard,' I wrote.

'That is not uncommon. Glance, in a casual manner, at her left hand.'

I glanced.

'It looks a bit stiff.'

'Precisely. She is afflicted with Dupuytren's contracture.'

'Is she?'

'She is.'

We got off the train at St Paul's. We walked about a mile, and then turned into the forecourt of a hospital.

'Did you practise here, sir?'

'I did.'

Doctor Cottie raised his hat several times as he led me along the tiled corridors. We arrived eventually at the matron's office. We entered. A tall, gaunt woman faced us. She winked at the doctor, tapped her nose with her index finger, and said 'Aha!'

'Aha!'

'Ah-haa!'

She slapped her thigh, and kicked a leg in the air. They beamed at each other.

'I should like, with your kind permission, dear Miss Medley, to show this bright young man the exhibits.'

'Of course you may. A medical student, is he?'

'He is indeed.' It was his turn to wink. 'After a fashion.'

'You still love your riddles, don't you, Doctor?'

They beamed again.

Matron Medley showed us into another room. She turned on the light and dozens of glass jars were revealed. They contained dead babies.

'Preserved in formalin,' the doctor explained.

'The five months' foetus is the most interesting,' the matron told me. 'I call him Stanley. I have names for all of them.'

During our third walk – from Cheapside to Leicester Square – I asked Dr Cottie why he had taken me to the hospital.

'In the midst of life, etcetera.'

'We are in death?'

'Precisely. I always felt a tingling sensation when I worked in the wards. You were excited – weren't you – seeing those tiny creatures?'

'No, sir. I thought I was going to be sick.'

'How surprising!'

We 'repaired to a modest place of refreshment for a light repast'. We ate smoked salmon beneath a large crystal chandelier.

'Your mother is a stern woman. So is the redoubtable Miss Medley. I admire women of a firm disposition.'

'Do you, sir?'

'They excite me, too, such women. They stir me.'

Our fourth walk was the longest. It took us from Piccadilly to the south-west of London. The doctor rushed ahead; I lagged behind – sweaty, morose, and near exhaustion.

'Come along, come along, Faint-heart.'

'I can't go any faster, sir.'

'The good Mrs Parkes will not be best pleased if we are tardy in arriving.'

'Who is Mrs Parkes, sir?'

'A force of nature. That is what she is.'

He stopped at the corner of a tree-lined street. When I caught up with him, he pointed to a mock-Tudor house, the front of which was almost obscured by a mass of white roses.

'Our destination. Get your breath back.'

'Thank you.'

'Your mother has misinformed me, it seems. According to her, you are an experienced pedestrian.'

'I am, sir. But I like to walk at a reasonable pace – if you don't mind my saying so.'

'Too fast for you, am I?'

'Yes, sir.'

'Emulate the tiger, not the snail. But to more urgent matters. Do not express surprise when Mrs Parkes addresses me by another name.'

'Yes, sir.'

'A man like myself – in medical circles something of a celebrity, I venture to suggest – has to cover his tracks.'

'I see, sir,' I said, although I didn't.

Attached to a bird-bath on the lawn was a sign, shaped like an arrow, pointing towards the house, on which the words 'Rose Bower' had been painted in Gothic lettering.

The doctor knocked at the front door three times.

'Is that you, Your Lordship?'

'It is. It is.'

A dumpy woman, tightly corseted, let us in. No 'Ahas' were exchanged.

'What a lovely day it is, Lord Leonard.'

'To be sure, Mrs Parkes.'

A 'force of nature' with a mauve rinse?

'Allow me to effect an introduction. Mrs Parkes, this is my—'

We waited.

'Your—?'

'My second cousin's great-nephew, the Honourable Peter,' he said, in a rush.

'Delighted to make your acquaintance. Are you partial to a nice cup of tea, like your—like your relative?'

'Yes, thank you.'

'Shall we take it in the lounge?'

'Rose Bower'—with its barometer and brass warming-pans in the hall, its floral-patterned carpets; its chairs and settees covered in chintz; its knick-knacks from the Far East; its smell of lavender polish—seemed a most unlikely setting for a 'force of nature'. If Mrs Parkes practised the black arts, I felt sure that she did so with the utmost refinement.

'Make yourselves comfy, won't you? Fifi and Pom-Pom, you're not to get under Lord Leonard's feet.'

A genuine 'force of nature' kept dogs like 'Gnasher' and 'Wolf', not a pair of freshly trimmed poodles.

'I'll be back in a jiffy, gentlemen.'

I tried to imagine Mrs Parkes at Wuthering Heights: I saw her perm disturbed as the daily gale swept through the building; I watched blood drip from her bangled wrist as it rubbed to and fro against the broken pane; I heard her say that she'd been a waif for twenty years …

'No time for day-dreaming.'

'No, sir.'

'I would advise you to make your choice while Mrs Parkes is engaged in the kitchen.'

'Choice, sir?'

He placed a photograph album on my knees.

'Choose a girl,' he said, abruptly.

'For—?'

'Precisely.'

I turned the pages. 'They all look very pretty,' I lied.

'You can't have them all. Not this afternoon, anyway. I would suggest that you – er – win their hearts – er – by degrees.'

'Well, this one, then.' She was a blonde called Rita.

'You have very good taste, obviously. I would not, however, recommend that undoubtedly charming young lady for – er – fun and games. She has Hutchinson's teeth. She carries no infection, but if I were you I would refrain from taking advantage of her – making use of her – good offices. It is better – is it not? – to be safe than sorry.'

'Yes, sir,' I replied, not understanding.

'Choose another.'

I chose. I chose wisely. Her name was Mabel. She had olive skin and dark-brown eyes. She undressed me slowly, kissing each part. Her tongue went everywhere, deliciously. My body, which I'd always loathed (it was a case containing my real self; a shell, nothing more), seemed beautiful now – it assumed a sheen, as she explored it; a silkiness.

The doctor thanked Mrs Parkes for the splendid Pekoe and the home-made scones ('I shan't partake, but my – er – relative will') and we left.

'How was it?'

I couldn't find adequate words. I told the doctor, truly, that I'd enjoyed myself.

'Mission accomplished, would you say?'

'Yes.'

'To your satisfaction?'

'Yes.'

'You will not – will you – inform your mother of the manner in which I disseminated the – I trust invaluable – knowledge you have acquired today?'

'No.'

'My explanation would have been a poor substitute. Let us avail ourselves of the first taxi that appears on the horizon. It is possible to over-exercise, and I have done so.'

In the cab, I asked him why he had described cosy Mrs Parkes as a force of nature.

'Because she is.'

'I thought she was very ladylike. She sounded ever so posh.'

'Camouflage.'

'She didn't look at all wild.'

'You haven't seen her in action. When she is concentrating on her duties, she is positively primeval.'

'So you know now, do you, You?'

'Yes, Mother.'

'I bet he took his time telling you, didn't he?'

'He did rather, yes.'

'Your father, you can rest assured, would have taken longer. At least you learnt about it from a proper doctor. Now, perhaps, you'll stop looking at diagrams.'

'I promise you, Mother, that I'll never look at another diagram again.'

'I should hope not. Your mind's morbid enough as it is, without those things adding to its troubles.'

I liberated Mother from her working clothes – a drab cotton frock, laddered stockings, 'sensible' shoes – and set her on a pink-sheeted bed where, with my long-dead father, she writhed ecstatically. I caught their moans.

'You're going to be arrested for staring at people one of these fine days.'

While I was learning how to add Lustre to the English stage, the doctor suffered a series of strokes and Mother was almost happy for a time.

An Attendant Lord

'No, he is not Prince Hamlet, nor was meant to be.'

'I think you may—'

'Of course I'm right. Only a prick like Hal Musgrave would have cast him in the first place.'

'You're Neville Drake, aren't you?'

'His shadow.'

'I'm Peter Smart.'

'Peter? It says "Hugh Smart" on the board.'

'I had to change my name when I entered the profession. It seems I share it with a juggler.'

'Christ, is he still with us? The poor old sod dropped every single one of his plates the last time I saw him. Just before you came in, I asked Mine Host if he had any champagne on the premises. He's scouring his cellar at the moment. He'll probably emerge with something tasting like Albanian goat's piss. If he does, will you share it with me?'

'That's very kind of you.'

'I'm not usually extravagant, but I really need to be given a boost, and champagne always does the trick. That read-through put me in the doldrums. Didn't you find it torture? If you've any pretensions to being half-way civilized, you have to agree.'

He was so certain of my answer that he didn't wait for it.

'Utter torture, as you say. Isn't this quite the most sordid public house you've ever been in? Those cheese sandwiches must have been prepared during Boadicea's reign. Even the flies are ignoring them. Total squalor.'

'I think the landlord's found a bottle.'

'So he has. Complete with cobwebs.'

Neville insisted on opening it with his own expert hands. He filled two pint glasses with warm champagne.

'Why did you choose "Hugh"?'

'It chose itself.'

'I see.'

A year passed before I was given the opportunity to explain what I meant. It was then I told him how my progress from 'You' to 'Hugh' had been swiftly accomplished.

'How do you judge people?'

'I try not to.'

'That remark doesn't bode well for our friendship. I hate wishy-washy liberals, absolutely hate them. You aren't seriously suggesting that the awful Hal didn't make any impression on you at all, are you?'

I thought for a minute or so. It was too long for Neville.

'You surely must have noticed that he ignored – studiously ignored, mark you – the ordinary social graces this morning. Did he introduce even one member of the company to another?'

'I –'

'Of course he didn't. It's part of his method.'

His look signified that he needed a cue. I provided it.

'Method?'

'Yes. He's playing at being a proletarian, dear. Hence the boorishness. For a dynamic young director, he has curiously old-fashioned ideas about how the plebs behave. He confuses directness with plain bloody rudeness. Did it strike your observant eye that he kept his cloth cap on throughout?'

'Yes.'

'What *about* that get-up? Those terrible old navvy's boots – it must take him at least an hour to untie the laces. Mind you, he probably sleeps in them. And those jumbo-size jeans – they've got more redundant material than a Walter Scott novel. The poor thing sees himself as a master of disguise, but he's ineradicably public school. Eton, I should imagine. Do you know how I judge people?'

'How?'

'By their underwear. I can tell at a glance if a person's knickers are fragrant. Yours are: his aren't. It's an infallible test: it cuts the world right down the middle. Which side of the fence are you on?'

'Sorry, I—'

'Sexually speaking. Men?'

I shook my head.

'Women, then?'

I smiled. 'What else?'

'You could flit from one to the other.'

'I don't think I do.'

'God, you're decisive. Have you found somewhere to live in this benighted hole?'

'Not really. I only arrived yesterday. I'm in a hotel.'

'Why don't you join me at Little Win's?'

'Where?'

'I can't guarantee that she'll accept you—she's very particular about who she has staying in her house. You'll have to be subjected to her scrutiny. I see no reason, though, why you shouldn't pass muster.'

'I'm not sure I—'

'Landlord, would you care to rummage in your basement again? This stuff will be the death of me, if I'm lucky. I must admit I do rather enjoy being extravagant every once in a while.'

'I may be one of the worst actors who ever drew breath, but at least I know I am. That's the difference between me and an old fart like Shir Shidney.'

'He hasn't been knighted yet, Neville.'

'He will be.'

Sidney Abbott, who played Claudius in Hal Musgrave's 'revolutionary' production of *Hamlet*, was nicknamed 'Shir Shidney' by Neville because of the intrusive 'h' he employed when performing Shakespeare:

'O wretched shtate! O boshom black ash death!
O limèd shoul, that shtruggling to be free,
Art more engaged; help, angelsh! Make asshay,

92

Bow shtubborn kneesh, and heart; with shtringsh of shteel,
Be shoft ash shinewsh of the new-born babe ... '

'God shpare ush. You are listening, Peter alias Hugh, to a voice
that was once compared to a cello. And quite rightly. Sidney's
all sound and no mind. He's an instrument, not a person. Ask
him for passion, and he obliges with his tremolo.'
  'If you think you're so bad, Neville, why do you go on?'
  'Don't misquote me. The awfulness of my acting is an in-
controvertible fact. I carry on because people want me to. You
like Wagner, of course?'
  'I'm not sure—'
  'Absolutely. He's marvellous, isn't he? When you visit me in
London, I'll play you my records. It's no exaggeration to say
that his music keeps me sane.'
  'You're being summoned, Neville.'
  'So I am. Heigh ho for another bracing encounter with
genius. Coming, Hal!'
Persistent self-denigrators are alarmed to hear their own
severe judgments confirmed by others. This simple truth was
revealed to me in the course of a frivolous conversation about old
films I had with Neville one night at Little Win's.
  'Did you ever see *They Flew to Glory?*' I asked.
  'Many times.'
  'Didn't you find it hilarious?'
  'Not particularly.'
  'Oh, you must have, Neville.'
  'I did not find it even remotely amusing.'
  'You couldn't have watched it with a straight face.'
  'But I did.'
  'The characters were so idiotically heroic.'
  'Not to me.'
  'You believed in them?'
  'Implicitly.'
  'I thought that you, of all people, would have laughed yourself
sick over that last scene in the cockpit.'
  'Then you thought wrongly.'
  'I've never heard you talk in that clipped manner before.'

'You are being quite insufferable.'

'In what way?'

'You know perfectly well. I was in *They Flew to Glory*. I didn't play a leading role, I admit, but my part was hardly negligible.'

'I don't remember you—'

'Flatterer.'

'Who were you?'

'The mechanic.'

'The mechanic?'

'The mechanic.'

'You played the mechanic?'

'No, I was the squadron leader's plucky little wife.'

'You were dreadful.'

'There are those who think otherwise.'

'Well, if you want my opinion—'

'I don't. I should want Nirvana before I wanted that.'

'As you please, then.'

'Dear God, I must have been deranged when I offered you my friendship. You're just as treacherous as the rest of them.'

'Neville?'

'The name is Drake. Really, it's utterly absurd that I should be sitting here in this hideous house in a town that has been aptly described as the arsehole of England, listening to the views of some tinpot actor whose talent—if any—has yet to be revealed—it is more than absurd, it is bizarre. I shall now go for a walk in the rain. The prospect of contracting pleurisy is to be preferred to another moment spent in your consummately charmless company.'

I was in bed when Neville returned. I heard Little Win tell him he looked like a drowned rat, only worse.

'It serves you right for chasing after your flibbertigibbets on a day of rest. You wet my clean stairs and there'll be trouble.'

He wished her sweet dreams.

'Charm never washed with me, so don't try using it.'

He knocked at the door of my room.

'Who is it?'

'Me.'

'Come in, Mr Drake.'

'Here. Have this.' He placed a bottle of brandy on the eiderdown. 'I was tetchy and petulant, and that is the extent of my apology. May I borrow a book?'

'Yes.'

'I can never sleep after a display of pique.'

'There isn't much of a selection. I didn't bring many with me.'

'I might have known, Hugh stroke Peter, that your taste in literature would be grimly highbrow. Culture, culture, culture — you've nothing here for a mere human to read.'

He took *With Stethoscope and Scalpel* from the shelf.

'What on earth is this?'

'The autobiography of an extraordinary man.'

'It looks lethally boring.'

'It is — and it isn't.'

'Are you recommending it?'

'It holds a special place in my affections.'

'You have them, do you?'

'I think so, Neville. Forgive me — Mr Drake.'

'I can't see myself curling up with anything else in your travelling library. By the way, it's my intention to be civil at breakfast.'

'Good night.'

'Good night.'

'Thank you for the present.'

'It's medicinal. It's to warm your piss.'

Number 23 Hyderabad Terrace was called Valencia, after the song.

'I've never set foot in Italy, and haven't any wish to from what I hear of the place. No, The Great Wilkie always used "Valencia" as his warming-up music.'

'Who was he?'

'Am I hearing you aright? Am I hearing your young friend aright, Mr Drake?'

'I'm afraid you are, Little Win.'

'The Great Wilkie was my father.'

'Oh?'

'He seems none the wiser, Mr Drake.'

'I fear you'll have to tell him, Little Win.'

'My father was The Great Wilkie, Mr —. What did you say your young friend's name was, Mr Drake?'

'Smart.'

'He doesn't appear to be — if a first impression is anything to go by. Anyhow, I'm The Great Wilkie's daughter. You're with me, are you?'

'Yes.'

'That's a relief, as the constipated duchess said when she got the wind up. That's one of his.'

'One of his what?'

'Your young friend isn't very quick on the uptake, is he, Mr Drake?'

'I'm afraid not, Little Win.'

'One of his jokes, that was. A duchess who's all clogged up inside surprises a burglar in her vestibule in the middle of the night. She gets the wind up and says "That's a relief!" He always had them rolling in the aisles with that one. Except in Sunderland, of course.'

'Why didn't they laugh in Sunderland?'

'It isn't known as the comedians' graveyard for nothing. No one laughs there. It's the climate. They opened what they have of their hearts to me, but then I was a novelty act, not a comic.'

'You were on the stage?'

'Was I on the stage? Did you hear what your young friend asked me, Mr Drake?'

'I did, Little Win.'

'He'll have to see my etchings — as the saying goes — won't he?'

'He will indeed.'

'I'll pardon your impertinence this once, Mr Smart. Yes, I was on the stage. I was famous for a while. I was a household name. The Great Wilkie and Little Win were the biggest draw on the halls when you were not so much as a twinkle in your daddy's eye.'

'Did you make jokes too?'

'Your young friend isn't much of a listener, is he, Mr Drake? Didn't I just say that I supplied the novelty?'

'What kind of novelty was it?'

'Shall I tell the young ignoramus, Mr Drake?'

'I would if I were you, Little Win.'

'Well, I started my act with six cart-wheels. One after the other, to a roll of drums. Then what do you think I did?'

'I can't imagine.'

'I stood on my head on a plinth.'

'It sounds incredible.'

'It was, believe you me. Guess what happened next.'

'I can't.'

'The Great Wilkie produced a trombone from his top hat – he was a conjurer as well, which I haven't mentioned – and stuck it in my mouth.'

'While you were upside down?'

'While I was upside down. Do you know, Mr Drake, there are times, even now, thirty odd years or more having passed, when I feel funny standing on my stockinged feet. It was well I stopped when I did or I'd never have got accustomed to not having my b.t.m in the air.'

'You didn't play the trombone, did you?'

'What the hell else do you think I did with it? There's not many things you can do with a trombone when you're on a plinth with your bloomers looking the world in the eye. I played "Abide With Me" and had the whole audience in tears. Even in Sunderland there was a sniffle or two.'

'I wish I'd seen you.'

'You'd have been amazed. Folk were. When the last note died away, you could hear a snail cough, I swear it.'

'Did you ever have to do an encore?'

'Your young friend asks some daft questions, doesn't he, Mr Drake? There were nights when my father, The Great Wilkie, had to call them to order, they were clamouring so. I'd give them the Trumpet Voluntary – pitched lower, of course – and "Onward, Christian Soldiers": it had to be something classical and inspiring because that was what I was known for. "You send them out with a glow, Little Win," the manager of

97

the Grand at Hartlepool used to say. "They come in here scum and they go out saints." It was nothing short of a miracle, according to him.'

'I'm sure.'

'I loved being asked for more, I won't deny. Any artiste worth her salt would, wouldn't she? It was when they insisted on a fourth number that I didn't relish it.'

'Why was that?'

'The day brains were distributed, you must have joined the queue for sawdust. It was my head — what else? You try standing on yours for fifteen minutes at a stretch and see what happens. I'd get this chronic throbbing if I went over my natural limit. My temples felt like they would burst open with all that blood rushing about inside. I'd have to be laid out in the wings with a cold compress — it was hours sometimes before I was back to normal. I've had a hard life, in many ways.'

I met with Little Win's approval. I was allowed to stay at Valencia.

'If you abide with me,' she said with a smile, 'it's under certain conditions. First, and foremost, I want no women — nor men either, come to that — in my rooms at night. Any sowing of wild oats goes on outside these premises. You're with me, are you?'

'Yes.'

'My second condition concerns the toilets. I keep two. One's upstairs; the other's in the rear garden. Both, naturally, are spotless. I've made it a rule at Valencia that the indoor toilet should gratify only liquid needs, if you follow me.'

'I do.'

'Last, but not least, is the matter of rent. Every Friday, thank you very much, on the nail, and no shilly-shallying. I never discuss financial business aloud, so I shall write the cost of board and lodgings on a piece of notepaper. If you find my terms unreasonable, then you're welcome to go elsewhere and pay more for less. And I don't respond to charm.'

'You don't?'

'No. Not at all. I don't, do I, Mr Drake?'

'No, Little Win.'

'He's for ever trying it on with me, and it gets him precisely nowhere. He fancies he can twist me round his little finger like he does with his flibbertigibbets. But he can't. The man hasn't been born who knows how to cast a spell over Little Win.'

'Really?'

'He looks frightened of me, Mr Drake – your young friend. It's all right, Mr Smart, I'm only human. Well, now that you've been made aware how the land lies, would you care for a guided tour of the old homestead?'

Photographs of Little Win, on and off her plinth, lined the staircase. 'My etchings,' she explained. I followed her up to 'the gods'. The Great Wilkie – rubicund, even in black and white – beamed down on us from the landing. A midget in Regency attire, The Pocket Beau Brummell, saluted a 'fellow little 'un' –

'God in His wisdom made us small
    Yet He knows – Win – that our hearts are Tall.'

'Fancied himself as a poet.'

My room looked out on the 'rear garden' – a red brick wall, two dustbins, a clutch of ragged robin, and the privy in which I could gratify my 'other than liquid needs'.

I asked Little Win why the yard in front of Valencia had been painted green.

'The front *garden*, if you don't mind. There was a lawn there once, but I had it taken up. It was too much trouble having it maintained, and pushing a mower across used to put yours truly's back right out of kilter. But when it was concreted over it looked so hard, I thought to myself "I can't stare out at *that* all day", so I got the builder to disguise it like. When the sun's full on it, you'd swear it was grass. It's cleaner, too – no creepy crawlies; no cats' mess. You should be snug in here.'

'Yes. I'm sure I shall be.'

'Come and see the bathroom. You're bound to be impressed.'

*

I was saddened when I read of Little Win's death a few months ago.

Dennis Andrew Miller, eighteen, unemployed, of no fixed address, was found guilty of the murder of Miss Winifred Lilian Desirée Collins, seventy-five, at the Central Criminal Court yesterday. He was sentenced to life imprisonment. In his summing up, the judge observed that Miller, who had been born and raised in the East End of London, had behaved in a manner that was all too typical of his class. Miller had sexually assaulted Miss Collins before strangling her.

As a young woman, Miss Collins was noted for the virtuosity with which she performed on the trombone.

I had kissed Little Win once.

'Give my cheek a peck—you have my permission. You're the cagiest person I've ever met.'

'Am I?'

'All locked inside yourself you are. Be a good boy now, and say goodbye, and write a nice message in my visitors' book.'

Her flesh, under a layer of white powder, on that cold November day, was strangely hot.

I remembered that heat, and shuddered.

' " … with a bare bodkin".'

'Congenital syphilis!'

'What's that you say, heart?'

'Congenital syphilis.' Hal Musgrave patted the tightly clenched hands of his psychiatric adviser. 'Dr Berry here thinks it's the reason why Hamlet is so unhappy.'

'I may be wrong, heart, but I thought, you know, that he was upset because, well, his father had been—it doesn't happen to many people—murdered.'

'Skin deep. Stop working on the surface.'

'But, heart, I mean, he does spend most of the play—you've got to agree—talking about it.'

Hal Musgrave removed his cloth cap.

'Danger signal,' whispered Neville.

'What am I trying to achieve in this production?'

'I don't know, heart.'

'I'm asking you.'

'Sod it, heart, I'm not a mind-reader.'

'Shall I tell you what I'm trying to achieve?'

'If you want to, heart.'

'The truth.'

'Sure, heart, I mean, you know, you must.'

'The fucking truth!'

'Yes, well, sure, heart.'

'The truth that bourgeois shit Shakespeare glossed over when he wrote this play. The truth he would have written if he'd had the guts.'

Hal Musgrave and Tony Woodhouse stared at each other. We waited.

'I mean, heart, I may be wrong, correct me if I am, but Hamlet's pretty messed-up as it is – I feel for the guy, you know, I do, honestly. Isn't giving him the pox piling it on a bit, heart?'

'Are you listening to this, Dr Berry?'

The doctor nodded vigorously.

'He thinks that Hamlet's messed-up. Pathetic, isn't it? He's about as messed-up, mate, as Rebecca of fucking Sunnybrook Farm. He's a prince. He has it made. The biggest problem he's got is verbal diarrhoea: "Shall I? Shan't I? Will I? Won't I?" What a pain in the arse.'

'The congenital syphilis, presumably,' whispered Neville.

'You said just now, heart, that he was unhappy.'

'So he was, but only marginally. He wasn't a peasant. He didn't have to work. His pain was a luxury.'

'You think that's all it was, do you, heart?'

Hal Musgrave started to bite the peak of his cloth cap.

'Heart?'

'Yeah?'

'How?'

'How?'

'How do I, you know, act it?'

'Act what?'

'Congenital syphilis. I mean, how do I convey, you know, to an audience, out there, without saying, that I've got the – like it's in the family – clap?'

Hal Musgrave pondered the question for several minutes.

'You could scratch yourself occasionally.'

'In the crotch?'

Dr Berry shook his head.

'Too obvious, Doc?'

Dr Berry nodded.

'A twitch now and then?'

'I can do a sort of tic, heart.'

'There must be recognizable symptoms.'

'Yes,' I said. 'There are.'

('The man approaching us has rhagades.'

'Sir?'

'Those scars by his mouth are rhagades.'

'How did he get them?'

'He inherited them, the poor wretch. One – or perhaps both – of his parents is culpable. See how pale he is.'

The stranger smiled nervously when Dr Cottie raised his hat to him.

'Hutchinson's teeth, as I suspected. A classic case.')

Thus it was that Tony Woodhouse became the first actor to play Hamlet with rhagades.

'When you walk on to that stage, the sight of you will scare the audience shitless.'

'But, heart, I mean, Ophelia, you know, finds him attractive, doesn't she?'

'Look, he's a prince, and she's a commoner. You follow me? She'd shove it his way if he had two heads.'

'What a way to spend one's life.'

Black rain fell steadily on Little Win's lawn.

'Purgatory can't be worse than a wet Sunday afternoon in a provincial town. Why on earth did I ever leave London?'

Neville supplied his own answer.

'It can't have been for money, and it certainly wasn't for love of my art. I think I was temporarily insane when I accepted the engagement. Oh Christ, now I've got indigestion. What *does* the erstwhile trombonist do to food to make it totally unpalatable? Subtle magic at the stove is decidedly not her forte. Have you taken a vow of silence?'

'I—'

'Or perhaps I bore you? I shan't wait for your reply; I'm in no mood to be castigated. I have seldom, if ever, felt so vulnerable. I intend to be extravagant this evening, and get spectacularly pissed. What else is there to do?'

Before I could think of the alternatives, he said:

'Where have I heard the names David Askew and Norman Machin? They seem to *sang* a distant *cloche*. Their case is all over the front page of our landlady's lurid paper.'

'What case?'

'I sometimes wonder which world you're living in. How could you have missed reading about the most hilarious trial in English legal history?'

'If you tell me what they've done, I'll tell you who they are.'

'Well, Peter alias Hugh, the intrepid pair have been supplying sheikhs and such with upper-class crumpet.'

'Do you mean the white slave trade?'

'So you *are* acquainted with the sins of the flesh, after all? Yes, my pale-faced celibate friend, that's exactly what I mean. It seems they've been dispatching the daughters of gentlefolk to the eastern hemisphere. In a just society, which ours isn't, they would be honoured for services to humanity, instead of being vilified by the gutter press.'

'They published Dr Cottie's memoirs.'

'The girls they transported in a drugged condition are called Fiona, Henrietta, Priscilla and Georgina—a sure indication that Askew and Machin are men of vision and not criminals. Since it's obvious from the supercilious expression you have chosen to adopt that my views on this subject are of no interest to you, I shall pretend I'm addressing them to someone else. I have this to say to him: the one Henrietta of my acquaintance had a voice so high and piercing that only dogs and bats could listen to her with any degree of pleasure. By removing four such defilers of our incomparable tongue to the confines of a far distant harem, Askew and Machin — may their tribe increase — have displayed an altruism one had hitherto suspected had altogether vanished from our midst. End of message to kindred spirit. Back to Valencia, a provincial Sunday, and you. Are you going to be polite enough to tell me who they are?'

'Askew and Machin?'

'No, dear. Jekyll and Hyde.'

'I've already told you.'

'When?'

'When you stopped for breath a few minutes ago.'

'I didn't hear you. Tell me again.'

'Listen carefully. They published Dr Cottie's memoirs.'

'Of course they did! I *knew* they were exceptional. So it's them we have to thank for the endless delights of *With Stethoscope and Scalpel*.'

'You enjoyed it, did you?'

'The word "enjoy", Peter dash Hugh, scarcely begins to describe the sensation, bordering on ecstasy, I experienced whilst reading the thoughts of that "humble medic". I have plans, Hugh or Peter, I have plans.'

'You have plans?'

'I have plans to appear in public disguised as F. Leonard Cottie. After six months capering as the First Player, it will be a new and exciting departure for me. I shall stand at a lectern, in a frock-coat, and pronounce the doctor's platitudes in oh such a sonorous tone: "Little did I know, as I sported on that famed shore whence Sir Francis and his stalwarts set forth, that one day I too should have my name inscribed — I speak, of course, figuratively — on Plymouth's Roll of Honour." By the way, what the hell are Malgaigne's bulgings?'

'I've forgotten.'

'Let me guess then. I picture some dingy, rat-infested Victorian tenement, deep in the heart of dockland. Sometimes the postman, protected by at least six policemen, delivers a letter: **A.** J. Fagin Esquire, 3a Malgaigne's Bulgings, Near Blackwall Way, E14. But they're probably something very ordinary, like adenoids.'

*

'Throw her on to the bed. Get on top of her. Let's see your arse going up and down.'

'But, heart, it seems, I mean, all wrong.'

'What's wrong about it?'

'She's his mother.'

'So?'

'So I don't think he'd do it. I mean, you know, why should he want to have it away with his mother?'

'There's a difference between having it away and rape. N'est ce pas, Doc?'

Dr Berry nodded.

'Rape did you say, heart?'

'That's what I said.'

'Why?'

'Why not?'

'Give me one good reason, heart.'

'Actors and their bloody reasons. It never occurs to them that human actions don't always have motives. Here's your reason, since you want one so badly. You've heard of penis envy?'

'Yes, sure I have, heart.'

'Well, Hamlet envies Gertrude's cunt.'

'He never says he does, heart.'

'Words, words — when are you going to forget them and *act*? If you wanted to fuck your mother, would you tell her? Where's your sense of repression? Show me the hidden Hamlet, the bloke who *senses* that Gertrude's got a great big powerful man-trap between her legs. She caught his father in it, and now Claudius is stuck. That's what Shakespeare meant to write but he chickened out.'

'Who said so, heart?'

'I say so. I know so. It's all there, throbbing away beneath the lines.'

'Is it, heart?'

'Yes, yes, yes, yes, yes! It's there, it's there, it's there!'

Hal Musgrave threw his cloth cap to the ground and stamped on it.

'No need to take on, heart. I mean, you know, I'm trying.'

'Prise it open.'

'Heart?'

'Violate it; bruise it; destroy it. Make sure that no one will get caught in it again.'

'I'll do my best, heart. Calm down, Hal. Shall we stop for tea first?'

That evening, Neville was gloomily prophetic:

'This production is so wilfully perverse that it has to be a success. Hal Musgrave will be hailed as a genius and our brain-damaged leading man will be praised for the acute intelligence of his conception. Dear God, I hate the theatre and all its works.'

He was delighted when the reviews confirmed his blackest forebodings:

Behold the Man

Last Tuesday night, on the stage of the Festival Theatre at ——, a major revolution took place. An old, dusty monument called *Hamlet* received a spring-cleaning from the hands of a certain Mr Hal Musgrave – a name that in two meteoric years has become synonymous with theatrical subversion of the most dynamic kind. Chipping away at the stonework with a chisel specially designed for the rehabilitation of public statues, Musgrave has chanced upon the man encased inside. Now he has applied artificial respiration, and with startling consequences.

Gone is the handsome, noble prince of popular legend; the romantic poet with the Rupert Brooke profile. In his place stands plain Mr Hamlet, a man among men, a commonplace neurotic. You would not be surprised to meet this Hamlet in a bus queue or at a football match. As personified by Tony Woodhouse, with his glowering presence and cawing voice, he comes across as an average psychopath whose very ordinariness strikes one as the most extraordinary thing about him.

For this revelatory production, Mr Musgrave has engaged the services of Maurice Berry, author of *The Splintered Mind*. Dr Berry's influence can be detected in the innumerable small, but telling, touches which make this *Hamlet* such a mind-stretching experience. In Musgrave and Berry's Elsinore the Ghost has a stammer; Polonius is a secret drinker; Laertes and Ophelia share a private sign language; and Gertrude—alternately smiling and weeping—is clearly going through the menopause. During the course of the play, Claudius washes his hands no fewer than thirteen times. Mere tragedy has been eschewed—what Musgrave and Berry confront us with is something very like the everyday world. To be shocked by their *Hamlet* is to be shocked by life itself.

And shocked, I confess, I frequently was. Watching Tony Woodhouse—a Hamlet prone to headaches and afflicted with sudden tics; his potato face pitted with acne—was like looking into a mirror and seeing one's private self revealed. This was the underground man and no mistake— here was Raskolnikov; here was Sartre's Roquentin; here was the archetypal loner in the grubby raincoat. His halitosis hit me in F6 of the stalls. As soon as he walked on last Tuesday, any notion that we would be witnessing the downfall of a Renaissance hero was immediately dispelled— listening, or rather *not* listening to Claudius's opening spiel, Woodhouse's gloomy Dane pointedly picks his nose. It is a tiny detail, but it sets the tone of the evening. The de-humanized stereotype, beloved of generations of theatre-goers, has been finally sent packing, and a real man has taken his place.

A catalogue of the miracles wrought by Hal Musgrave (and his 'psychiatric adviser', as the programme denotes Maurice Berry) would take me a week to prepare. Let me single out for mention the way in which he has coped with the servant problem at Elsinore. No longer are we asked to watch a group of spear-carriers waiting for the leading actors to be stricken with some fatal disease so that they can assume the roles and dazzle us accordingly. Instead, we are invited to witness the unlikely spectacle in a Shakespeare production of people actually *working*. I have never before seen such busyness on an English stage, so much genuine activity. Musgrave's skivvies speak (without words) for countless generations of oppressed human beings: they know, even as they scrub and polish, and bow and scrape, that their descendants will one day inherit the earth. In the interval last Tuesday, I looked about me at the well-dressed first-night audience and wondered how many of them had realized that a Marxist director was telling them their whole way of life was rotten. As they went on drinking and brightly chattering, I felt tears of frustration pricking at my eyes.

If I have a complaint to make, it's with Shakespeare, the last scene of whose play proves almost too much for a master of realism like Hal Musgrave. Not even he can tidy up convincingly the playwright's loose ends. But that is to cavil. This is, blow by blow, a peerless production. I very much doubt that I could love anyone who wasn't stirred, moved and ennobled by it.

'I don't know about you, but reading that has brightened my Sunday. The best, however, is yet to come. The critic employed by the other posh paper has written an article of quite exceptional perverseness.'

'What does he say?'

'Absolutely nothing about Mr Woodhouse.'

'Are you serious?'

'I am. He was more impressed by the actor playing Reynaldo.'

'But that's me.'

'Is it? I didn't recognize you from his description. Read him, and marvel.'

I read, and what I read I marvelled at, after a fashion:

In Mr Hal Musgrave's admirable production of *Hamlet* at —————— there is one moment of undeniable splendour. It was St Augustine who observed in Book XIII of his majestic work *Concerning the City of God against the Pagans* that only those human beings who continue in perfect obedience will be granted the immortality of the angels and an eternity of bliss. It says much for Mr Hugh Smart's performance as Reynaldo that I was inextricably reminded of the great saint's coruscating insight when he spoke, with an almost defiant simplicity, the three words 'Good, my lord.' As uttered by Mr Smart, they took on a quality I have no hesitation in calling religious. It was like hearing a trumpet sound.

But a muted one. Mr Smart's Reynaldo is not a man to whom braying comes naturally. His is a still small voice; a voice that says, with a quietude that brings to mind the peace that passeth all understanding, three monosyllabic words: 'Good, my lord.' A lifetime's servitude is conveyed, effortlessly. Beyond Polonius, Mr Smart suggests, is God Himself – He to whom all obedience is due. Mr Smart's Reynaldo will carry a father's message to Laertes, but for God's sake. 'Good, my lord,' he says, in a single breath – a breath that dies in the air like the last note of a Beethoven quartet. We sense, even as we listen, that the word 'lord' is addressed to two masters – one on earth, the Other in Heaven. Mr Smart's Reynaldo is giving faithful service to them both. Not for nothing did I think of St Augustine.

Mr Smart's 'Good, my lord' ranks with the finest moments in modern theatre. As his Reynaldo set off with calm determination, I recalled that cold December night in 1947 when Eloise Ferrat made the audience sweat with her in André Bisset's undeservedly forgotten *Chez Myrtle* at the Théâtre ———. 'Qu'il fait chaud' said Mme Ferrat, fanning herself with an air-mail edition of *Le Monde*. I remember quite distinctly loosening my tie, such was the power of Mme Ferrat's acting. Her 'Qu'il fait chaud' suggested not only excessive tropical heat, but a lifetime's irritation with the weather. 'Qu'il fait chaud' said Mme Ferrat with an exquisite weariness, and suddenly we were in a brothel somewhere in French colonial Africa, waiting – like her – for the cool evening breezes to bring our flesh a fleeting tranquillity. I thought, too, of that scene in *The Basement Area* when Beryl Masters, as Mary, carefully peeled off her surgical stocking and asked – with a heart-breaking expectancy of receiving the customary answer to an oft-repeated question – 'Am I really in Stockport, Eddie?' There was a pause before Mr Russell Clive, playing the brutish Eddie, said 'Yes' – a pause that seemed to stretch into eternity, as

Miss Masters looked at him with a quivering intensity expressive of a still unvanquished hope. 'Yes' said Mr Clive, and then – slowly, pitifully – the trace of a smile broke on Miss Master's face: 'That's good.' With two words, Miss Masters caused wonder to radiate about her. Her softly voiced 'That's good' turned Stockport into Illyria. At that moment, everyone in the theatre wanted to be with Mary in Stockport. It was nothing less than a primal need.

I shall go again to ——— in the certain expectation of Mr Smart's 'Good, my lord' falling on me like soothing balm.

'You historic little thing, you. You must be the first Reynaldo to steal the show from The Moody. I can't believe it's ever been done before.'

'But St Augustine –'

'Oh, he's a regular in Mr Puff's column. Though I seem to recall that Thomas à Kempis once ousted him for a few weeks. Before you consider charging us lesser mortals a penny to talk to you, let me remind you that the three most useless things in the world are the Pope's balls and a good notice from that gentleman.'

'It's incredible.'

'It even amazed me. Laertes I could understand (though not our one); Ophelia I could understand (though not our one); my own highly original interpretation of the First Player I could understand completely – but Reynaldo!'

'You're jealous, Neville.'

'Say them for me.'

'Say what?'

'Those three magic words.'

' "Good, my lord." '

'Well?' I asked, breaking a long silence.

'I'm undecided. I thought I *just* caught the sound of a far-away trumpet – muted, of course – but on balance I feel that the comparison with the last note of a Beethoven quartet is more apt. Would I be on the right track if I said I detected the faintest hint of the Rasumovsky?'

*

So the man who had yearned to be Hamlet became – for one critic, at least – the definitive Reynaldo.

I was never happy playing him. Once on the stage, I wanted only to be off again. The comforting gloom of the wings was my goal: I threw myself into it at every performance with 'calm determination'. But before I reached that dark haven the thumping of my heart made me deaf to Polonius's instructions. I read his lips, and spoke. Panic possessed me; sweat suffused me. Then, at long last, the moment came. My knees positioned for escape, I sounded my muted trumpet, emitted my dying fall, and fled.

I felt ridiculous in doublet and hose. In baggy tights, I looked like a stick insect with dropsy. The case that contained my real self seemed to wither in that glare. The audience mocked it with silent laughter.

To my astonishment, I found myself making fun of the play that had once stirred me so profoundly in Dr Cottie's Temple of Wisdom. At Neville's instigation, I scanned the text for Additional Characters. He himself suggested an Irish insurgent, called in by the Prince to help upset the *status quo* ('Now might I do it, Pat'.) Each night, after my ordeal, the cast-list grew: Art Prithee, the saxophonist; Lug the Guts, an obese Welshman; Han(d)s Apt, the Flemish artist; Madam Ho, a Chinese laundress; Neighbour Room, that friendly yokel, who occasionally visited Madam Come's brothel, where he had a delicious quickie with Felicity Awhile, from whom – such was her popularity – he was soon absented; the flatulent priest, Father Grossly ('full of bread') ... There were many more.

Out of my weakness and my melancholy, I courted the absurd. Very little in life seemed worthy of serious consideration. The little there was I hoarded up, I hoped: it was a rock, of sorts; I could build on it, one day.

After my ordeal each night, after 'Lug' and 'Art', I went down to that dark haven, the wings, where I watched Walter Latham assume the character of the First Gravedigger. It was a consummate assumption: the words, the snatches of songs, came from the lips of a countryman, not an actor. I had seen such men at the farm in my childhood, their faces reddened by the weather and beer. They spoke in short bursts, and always about practical matters. Walter's old clown was of their useful number. His graveyard was his pride: each rotten corpse was known to him; each scattered bone, one felt, might inspire a story—some recollection of long-past lechery, perhaps, that could still excite living flesh. He was at home in the earth. 'Come, my spade!', he said, spitting on the metal and polishing it with his sleeve, 'there is no ancient gentlemen but gardeners, ditchers and grave-makers—they hold up Adam's profession', and down he went, smiling, into Ophelia's grave. Nothing I have seen or heard in the theatre has ever moved me as much as that confident boast.

Cunningly contrived (though neither cunning nor contrivance was visible), Walter Latham's acting appeared to be as natural as breathing. It burgeoned before one's eyes: it suggested, with a rugged delicacy, a much richer life than the mere extract one was privileged to witness. In Hal Musgrave's 'revolutionary' pro-duction of *Hamlet*, Walter's unnamed delver was the 'King of infinite space', not the tic-afflicted Prince.

So sane on stage, so wise, so humorously observant, Walter's life beyond it was a wretched business. His torture chamber opened twice daily and had as many disguises as it had names—The Rose and Crown, The Nag's Head, The Queen's Arms. His whips and manacles were double whiskies and pints of Guinness, consumed in earnest in strict rotation. Walter's destruction was quietly willed.

His art was similarly disciplined. It was perfectly timed, though not in clockwork fashion: you couldn't see the workings. What his gift allowed you to see was something denied to the 'regulars' of The Rose and Crown, etcetera—a soul, a spirit; call it what you will. It survived his body's decay, his mind's befud-dlement. It had an unassertive authority.

One day, over a 'wet' lunch, I asked him how he did it. He glared at me. He commanded the barmaid to pour me a large Scotch.

'How do I do *what*?'

'Your—'

'My?'

'Your—'

'My? My? Tell me what it is while I've still got breath inside me.'

'Your acting.'

'I do it because I can't do anything else. I'm stuck with it for good and all because it comes easily to me.' He lifted his glass. 'And it pays for this.'

No sensible man, he said, would want to spend his life acting. Only fools trod the boards: the half-formed, the insecure, the downright childish. No man in his senses would choose to waste his time listening to the bilge actors spewed out.

'I haven't met one with a brain yet. The ones who think they're brainy are the worst. They usually can't act either. Oh, they talk a load of Stanisbloodylavski bullshit about "truth", but that's where their intelligence begins and ends. Actors would be the lowest of the species if there weren't such things as directors to beat them to the bottomless pit by a head. Just thinking about them gives me a thirst.'

I paid for his next pint. He thanked me.

'I flew.'

'Sorry, Mr Latham, I don't understand.'

'Aeroplanes. When I was living. Before the rot set in. I was the youngest pilot in the squadron. The sodding Boche shot me down.'

My father's green face hovered above our glasses. I blinked it away.

'Kraut doctor operated on me. Put a metal plate in my skull. That finished me for flying. I never went up again.'

Yes, he said, his real life had come to an end in Germany. Acting had been a poor substitute since. Besides, any idiot could do it; whereas it took real skill, real concentration, to guide a plane through the air. He talked of nerve, discipline, courage. They were qualities, I told him, I recognized in his art.

'Piss off.'

'No.'

'Have another Scotch then.'

'Yes.'

Walter spoke deprecatingly of his long career. His early, legendary performances were quickly dismissed: 'The past. They've gone. Words won't bring them back.'

I asked him about his future. He smirked.

'You should play King Lear.'
'Too many lines. The Gravedigger's my limit these days.'

Dr Cottie, almost gaga in London, never heard my muted trumpet; never saw the Lustre I added to the English stage. It was just as well. Before I arrived at my definitive Reynaldo, I played—in various parts of the country—several detectives ('Where were you, Your Ladyship, at precisely 10.46 p.m. on the evening of the 24th?'); several victims ('You realize, of course, that this is blackmail?') and several characterless by-standers ('The boot! The boot is poisoned!'). I doubt that I was ever convincing.

'Hullo, Mother.'

'Oh, it's you, is it? I thought you were supposed to be up there among the heathens.'

'It's Sunday today.'

'I can still tell which day of the week it is without your assistance, thank you very much.'

'There's no performance on Sunday. I decided to come home for a change. I caught the six o'clock train this morning.'

'I didn't imagine you got here on wings.'

'How's the doctor?'

'Any other son would ask how his mother was first.'

'How are you, Mother?'

'Look at the back of my hand.'

My 'What?' received the inevitable reply.

She thrust her right hand at me.

'Just look.'

'I can't see anything. What should I be looking for?'

'You'd soon see if you had them, You.'

'Them?'

'Liver spots!'

'Where?'

'Here.'

A brown speck was barely visible.

'You know what that means, don't you?'

'No.'

'It means I'm over the hill. It means I'm on the way down.'

'Down?'

'One of these fine days, you'll understand what I'm talking about. Liver spots are the first sign of old age. The best years of my life have gone.'

'Oh, Mother, how can you say that?'

'Because it's the truth. I've been nothing but a slave since I was daft enough to marry your father. Then there was you to feed and clothe and keep sensible. Then there was Him upstairs with his airs and graces and God knows else what.'

'What else.'

'Trust you to correct me. I said to myself when I read that stuff about you in the paper, I said "This is bound to alter his hat size, this is," I said.'

'You read the review?'

'No, I dreamt it. I suppose you think you're God's gift to the stage now. It was all in the air to me, the stuff that man wrote about you—I can't say I made any sense of it.'

'Neither did I.'

'You don't have to pretend to be a modest little flower for my benefit, You.'

'I'm serious, Mother. Believe me.'

'I wonder.'

'You've never read that newspaper before.'

'No. And I'll never read it again, if I can help it.'

The doctor should have looked pitiful, but didn't. His mouth was twisted to one side and his limbs useless, yet his eyes were defiantly bright and energetic. They knew who I was; they spoke my name; they gave me the warmest of welcomes.

He lived in the library, in a wheelchair. These days, more cheerfully, Mother satisfied his very different requirements.

'I've caught the old fool crying a few times,' she said, slightly smiling, when we left him to sleep. 'Unawares.'

I took hold of Sebastian's arms.

'That thing! Him in there was always morbid, like most of the people I've had dealings with. And you're the same. Let go of it.'

'The doctor introduced us years ago.'

'I'm sure he did. I can just see him doing it. I've come to the conclusion, thinking things over lately, that I'm about the only sane person in the world.'

'You could be right.'

'Sarcastic as ever, aren't you, You?'

Mother scowled when I opened a bottle of wine to drink with dinner.

'I can tell what circles you're moving in. Your father contented himself with beer.'

'Can I tempt you to a glass?'

'You try.'

'You might enjoy it.'

'My system's bad enough as it is without adding poison to it.'

Every sip I took provoked an exclamation from her – 'Hm!', 'Tt!', 'Well!', 'Ugh!'

She coughed, as was her custom, when we finished eating.

'I'll be back in London in December, Mother.'

'Thanks for the warning.'

'But I shan't be living here.'

'Too small, is it?'

'No.'

'I should hope not.'

'I want,' I said, surprising myself, 'to live my own life.'

'Whose have you been living all these years, then?'

'I want a bit of freedom.'

'If you're locked up in chains, I can't see them from where I'm sitting.'

'A friend called Neville Drake has offered me a room in his flat. A choreographer has it at the moment, but he'll be moving out soon.'

'Is that someone medical?'

'No. A choreographer is a person who creates ballets.'

'Ballets? Do you mean dancing?'

'Yes, Mother.'

'Good God! You watch yourself, You. You be careful.'

'Why should I be careful?'

'You ought to know by now, with your so-called education.

What you do as an excuse for a proper job – gallivanting about in old-fashioned clothes, and spouting nonsense – would make decent people shudder if they saw you at it, but ballet dancing! Grown men running after girls got up as swans and worse – it doesn't bear thinking of. Tell me his name.'

'The choregrapher's?'

'We weren't, as far as I recall, discussing anyone else.'

'Serge Evanowski.'

'A foreigner.'

'Actually, he's Welsh. From Cardiff.'

'Just as bad. Nearer home, I grant you, but almost as difficult to cope with. A Welshman's all right when he's singing, but not otherwise.'

'I'll come and see you whenever I can.'

'Honoured, I'm sure. I'd drop you a curtsy if my legs weren't so stiff. Don't exert yourself for my benefit.'

'Will you move to a smaller place when he dies?'

'He'll probably see me out. I'm certain he will. It would be typical of him. He'll cling on – helpless as he is; in that damned chair – long after me. I'm bound to go first. Some other person will get his money.'

Neville disgraced himself on two occasions during the last week of the run of *Hamlet*.

The first disgraceful act took place in Little Win's bathroom. His firm refusal to gratify 'other than liquid needs' in the outside toilet, in torrential rain, at three in the morning, resulted in the Valencian shrine being desecrated.

'I thought I informed you, Mr Drake, that that bowl was not to be used for solids.'

'I don't see why I should brave the elements simply to have a shit.'

'You know quite well that I keep an umbrella by the back door. You wouldn't have got wet.'

'It's colder than a nun's fanny in Lent out there. I prefer to crap in comfort, thank you.'

'Not on the best Royal Doulton china.'

'Are you mad? What do you think that thing was designed for? Flower arrangements?'

I joined them at the scene of the crime.

'Rasy' – such was my new name; it was short for Rasumovsky – 'this lunatic here is railing against me for answering a call of Nature.'

'He dropped solids, Mr Smart, where I asked him not to.'

'There's no trace of them left.'

'I can see them in my mind's eye, though. That's what hurts.

The sharp whiteness of Little Win's features vanished as we stood there, shivering. Grey tracks slowly blurred it.

'I've cherished that for years. I've always kept it shining and sweet-smelling. I must have put gallons of eau-de-cologne in it. It was fit for royalty to look at before he went and dirtied it.'

Neville, witnessing something absurdly like sorrow, apologized.

'It's no good now. What's done is done. I'm glad you're going soon. I couldn't have borne you staying longer.'

Five nights later, Neville disgraced himself before eight hundred people. They were less amazed than the diseased prince when the First Player suddenly became inexplicably belligerent. Hamlet's advice, in that closing performance, was not accepted with gratitude:

HAMLET. Speak the speech I pray you as I pronounced it to you, trippingly on the tongue —
IST PLAYER. I beg your pardon?
HAMLET. ... but if you mouth it as many of your players do —
IST PLAYER. What did you say?
HAMLET. ... I had as lief, I mean, the town-crier spoke my lines ...
IST PLAYER. Could you possible speak up?
HAMLET. ... spoke my lines. Nor do not saw the air —
IST PLAYER. Are you addressing *me*?
HAMLET. Heart?
IST PLAYER. I asked you, quite distinctly, if you were addressing me.
HAMLET. ... do not saw the air with your hand thus, but use all gently, for in the very torrent, tempest, and as I may say

whirlwind ... Stop staring at me like that, heart.

1ST PLAYER. How dare you tell me how to act!

HAMLET. O, it offends me to the soul, to hear a robustious
periwig-pated fellow tear a passion to tatters —

1ST PLAYER. You must hate yourself in that case.

HAMLET. Shut up, for Christ's sake, will you? I mean, you know,
it nearly bloody kills me, playing this part. Get off my back,
and stop pissing around. Now where the hell was I? Let me
think. (Clicks his fingers several times; scratches his head;
adjusts his tights at the crotch, and says —) As I was saying, be
not too tame neither ...

The play continued without further textual amendments. In the
interval, Neville received a black eye from Tony Woodhouse,
and a shtream of inventive abushe — declaimed in his besht voiche
— from 'Shir Shidney'.

' "Safely stowed." Home at last. O London, lovely London! O
putrid, precious Paddington! Don't listen to me, Rasy, while I
wax lyrical. An occasion like this, I think, calls for a little
extravagance. I'll just nip down to our friendly neighbourhood
vintner and pick up a few bottles of the Widow Clicquot's un-
surpassed beverage. In the meantime, make yourself — as they say
— comfy. You'll find my boudoir at the end of the passage.'

Neville's bedroom belonged to Wagner. The composer, in
marble, stared at himself, in bronze: the marble face wore a
furious expression; the bronze one looked smug. Marble raged
at one end of a plush maroon chaise-longue; Bronze beamed
back at him from the other. An entire wall was covered with
photographs of scenes from productions of the operas: dumpy
heldentenors fought with dragons, forged swords, or boarded
swans; abundant sopranos reclined — in postures approximately
suggestive of imminent rapture — on rocks.

I opened the score of *Lohengrin* and a photograph of a very
different master fell out. It showed him dressed against the cold,
playing cards with someone unseen. 'À mon ami, Neville — André
Gide,' ran the inscription.

Neville returned with a case of champagne.

'I've bought enough for the week. I intend to be euphoric for at least seven days. I know now how Florestan felt after his release. Allow me this one indulgence.'

'You never told me you knew André Gide.'

'You've been rummaging, obviously. I see I shall have to lock my door before I leave you alone in the flat. Yes, I met him once.'

'How?'

'Fill my glass and I'll tell you. When I was fifteen or so – I can't recall the exact age – a would-be seducer of my young self lent me a copy of Gide's *Corydon*. You're familiar with the book, of course?'

'No.'

'Quelle surprise! Well, Rasy, I read it and was overwhelmed. That brave old paederast immediately became my hero. If he didn't feel guilty above loving boys, why – I reasoned – should I?'

'When did you meet him?'

'I went to France, on my ownsome, one summer holiday. At the time, it seemed more like a pilgrimage than a trip. I wrote to him, and to my immense surprise received an invitation to tea. I rushed to the nearest chemist and bought a large bottle of liquid tan.'

'I'm mystified.'

'My skin has never turned brown.'

'I'm still mystified.'

'Exposed to the sun, it goes a nasty lobster colour.'

'What has this to do with André Gide?'

'He had a penchant for Arabs.'

'And you wanted to look Arabian?'

'Yes. But I succeeded in looking grotesque instead. The great man visibly blanched as I tippytoed into his study. Dear God, the embarrassment I must have caused him. He offered me his hand, I remember, rather warily – it was as if he'd anticipated that something nasty was about to happen to it. Something nasty did. My sweaty palm met his dry one and stained it with a bloody great dollop of *Monsieur Soleil*.'

'Did he recoil in horror?'

'No. He laughed.'

'That was good of him.'

'Yes, it was. I'm amazed that a cold fish like you could be so perceptive: it was *very* good of him. His was the kindest laughter I've ever heard.'

'You sound drunk.'

'I couldn't be more sober, or more serious. Shall I continue?'

'Please do.'

'Actually, there isn't much more to tell. I was in such a frenzied state of admiration, I scarcely heard what he said. I know he told me to read Dostoevsky.'

'And did you?'

'I tried to, but gave up. I found him far too earnest, far too turgid. I'm afraid I left some of my counterfeit tan on the arm of his sofa.'

'Dostoevsky's?'

'Do you find it necessary to be flippant about everything?'

'With you, yes.'

Hours passed before my apology was accepted.

While I lived in the room in which Serge Evanowski had thought up such seminal ballets as *Ecloques IV* and *Pensées Beiges*, I found it necessary to be flippant about almost everything. That serious part of me – my rock, of sorts – I kept hidden from Neville. Like a miser counting his gold. I examined it in solitude. I couldn't risk contamination.

I was in Limbo. I knew I was. Flippancy seemed appropriate.

'You're an iceberg, you know.'

'Am I, Neville?'

'I've no reason to think otherwise. I have yet to hear you express an impassioned opinion on any subject worth talking about.'

'You're shouting.'

'Have you ever been in love?'

'Have *you*?'

'That's my concern. Are you going to answer?'

'You're turning purple.'

'And you are a fucking eunuch.'

'Isn't that a contradiction in terms?'

'You really are odious. Why don't you stand up for yourself? Why don't you lose your temper? Why don't you hit me for insulting you?'

'It isn't in my nature.'

'Why don't you change it then? It could only be for the better.'

'Yet another grey hair! With any luck, I'll be bald in a couple of years.'

'You sound happy at the prospect.'

'I am, Rasy. I shall inspire complete confidence when I have a shiny bonce.'

'With whom?'

'Mit meinen jungen Freunden, natürlich.'

'I don't see how.'

'German boys are taught to respect their elders. Ergo — the older I look, the more likely am I to succeed with them. Do you think I'm wicked?'

'Of course not.'

'What a pity. You'd be a much more interesting person if you were occasionally intolerant. Tell me I'm corrupt.'

'I can't, Neville.'

'Please say I shock you.'

'I can't, Neville, because you don't. Certain aspects of your character intrigue me, though.'

'Do they?' Grinning, he dropped to his knees before me. 'Name just one of them, Rasy, I beg of you.'

'Well, why is it only Germans you chase after?'

'How tactfully expressed. I can answer you in a sentence. Because I enjoy mastering the master race.'

'I didn't realize there were quite so many of them in London.'

'Ah, but then *I* know where to look. I find those lederhosened lads wherever Culture manifests itself. Like the National Gallery, for instance. That's my hunting-ground throughout the summer. I haunt the place — the Italian rooms, in particular. The Renaissance — after years of swatting up on Burckhardt, Berenson *et al* — has become my speciality. Germans are suckers for erudition, in more ways than one: drop a few names like Piero, Masaccio and Filippo Lippi and you're halfway there. "The Virgin of the Rocks" has been a godsend to me.'

'In what way?'

'Dear bloodless Rasy, you can always be relied upon to rise to the bait. The painting is protected by glass. You can see your reflection in it, and—much more interestingly—the reflections of others. I smile hesitantly; he smiles back—perhaps; we speak, and then I set about dazzling him with my knowledge. Lunch follows, or dinner—depending on the time of day. What happens next I prefer not to mention, for propriety's sake.'

'Thank you for considering my feelings, Neville.'

'I once picked up an American of Prussian descent out of desperation. The moment orgasm was achieved, he clasped his hands together and began to pray.'

'To God?'

'No, to Mom. He asked her to forgive him for the wicked sin he had just committed. Tears of shame coursed down his face. I gave him very short shrift, I assure you. He called me Satan as he left.'

Wagner, in joyous mood, boomed from Neville's bedroom when it was graced with the presence of Fritz, Rudi, Joachim or Heinrich. The Mastersingers sang, and sang. And sang. When, however, he returned to the flat alone—which was most days, despite his boasting—he would slam every door, break the odd plate, smash a glass or two, and shout insults at me: I was an asexual turd; a hole in the air; a zombie. Then he would listen to the Liebestod, or Siegfried's Funeral Music, or the whole of *Parsifal*.

One morning—after a night made restless by too frequent reminders that the citizens of old Nuremberg had been possessed of the competitive spirit—I awoke to find a naked stranger looking down at me.

'I am Wolfram,' he said.

'How do you do?'

'I am well. I am fit, and blooming too. You are Mr Neville's friend?'

'Yes.'

'You are Mr Neville's *special* friend?'

'No.'

'I am glad. I am happy for you. Mr Neville I do not care for.'

'You don't?'

'I do not indeed. He is truly terrible. He I met in your British Museum. I am by Assyrian art quite fascinated. Are you?'

'I don't think so.'

'Then you do not lies tell, like Mr Neville. He speaks whoppers —you see, I your slang words am acquainted with. What, please, is your name?'

'Hugh. No, it's not. I'm still sleepy, I'm afraid. I'm Peter.'

'And I am Wolfram.'

I sat up. We shook hands briskly.

'Mr Neville played me the music of Wagner. Wagner I do not like. I prefer myself your Tin Pan Alley. All English do not your Shakespeare love. I am a German who with Wagner is considerably very much fed up.'

'Is Neville asleep?'

'No, Peter, he has to act in a film gone.'

'Oh yes, I'd forgotten.'

'He is not a famous film star, I think?'

'No, he's not.'

'He said you would a hearty breakfast cook for me. Your worldwide famous ham and eggs. Tea and toast and marmalade. Just this minute I have an appetite for other things. If you to the window move, I the space will have to keep you company. Please?'

I moved towards the window. He joined me in the bed.

'I would much like for us to make love. You are my type. Your eyes and nose and mouth attract me. Mr Neville and I did not ourselves enjoy. He is a strange man. He wanted to—what is the word when you do not fight but still attack each other?'

'Wrestle.'

'Quite so. He requested me to wrestle with him across the carpet. I did not wish, so he played the music of Wagner louder.'

We kissed.

No, I said to myself, no, this mustn't happen; I don't want life to be so complicated. No, no, no, no, no.

124

We kissed again.

As I entered him, I thought: I shouldn't be doing this. After all, I'm a man. Tits excite me, and I'm cunt-struck, too. Yes, I am. I am definitely cunt-struck.

I stopped thinking.

But not for long: stroking Wolfram's cropped blond hair, I saw a tree in a country garden and a boy standing beneath it.

'Harvest.'

'You are squeezing the breath out of my body, Peter.'

'Forgive me.'

'I enjoy, but not so much to feel like a fish on a beach.'

For a moment, his warm flesh smelled of apples.

(Granny Smart polished them on her apron before they went into the basket:

'That Jerry hasn't altered their flavour, our Pete. A bird's had a peck at this one — you can eat up what the little blighter didn't get at.')

'You are eating me, Peter. I enjoy, but not with such strength from the teeth.'

We had breakfast in the late afternoon.

'I will write to you, Peter, and you must to me communicate as well. You will stay with me when you to Darmstadt come. My mother is a good cook, and I have two beautiful sisters and my father last year purchased for our family your English King Charles spaniel. He is a merry little scamp.'

I slept contentedly after Wolfram's departure. Neville woke me.

'Have you been in bed all day?'

'No.'

'Did you meet that German boy?'

'You mean Wolfram?'

'Oh, I can't remember his name. He was wonderful between the sheets, Rasy.'

'Was he, Neville?'

'I don't mind being insulted by my superiors — by artists — but to be put down by a mere bank manager!'

'He's rude, is he?'

'The tone of his letter is that of someone addressing an imbecile. I am not an imbecile.'

'No, Neville.'

'Am I an imbecile?'

'I just said you weren't.'

'I'm so enraged I didn't hear you. If he *has* to remind me that I owe the piffling sum of ten pounds, he could at least pay me the compliment of not couching his reminder in the language of the nursery. Sod him and all his kind. Spiritual values are unknown to them.'

I didn't see the connection between spiritual values and his debt to the bank. I said so. The observation went unheard.

'This other one looks like a bill. I shan't open it.'

'Let me.'

'If it *is* a bill, just nod, and in heaven's name don't tell me how much it's for. Anything to do with money sickens me.'

'Does it really, Neville?'

'You know it does. My nerves are in a terrible state.'

'I can't believe you'll be sickened by this. It's a cheque for two hundred guineas.'

'For me?'

'For you. A television series you appeared in has been sold to an American network.'

'We'll have champagne tonight, Rasy. If I survive this morning's ordeal, that is.'

'What ordeal?'

'Haven't I told you?'

'Obviously not. Why else would I ask?'

'An income tax inspector is visiting me at eleven. What time is it now?'

'Just after nine.'

'Then we must put the plan into action straight away.'

'What plan?'

'You *will* help me with it, won't you?'

'If I knew—'

'You can't refuse.' He looked at me menacingly. 'No true friend would.'

'Tell me my duties.'

All his belongings – everything except his bed, and a Bible held together with Scotch tape – were to be shifted upstairs, to the flat owned by that blue-haired old bitch, the Honourable Mrs Forbes, whose aged, mottled and totally uninviting flesh was currently being exposed to view on one of the Canary islands, to the alarm no doubt of the residents, and the keys to which (the flat, Neville reminded me) were in his possession.

'I shall be pleading poverty.'

Accompanied by shouts of 'Do hurry, please!' and 'Get a move on!', I transferred most of Neville's portable property to the wealthy widow's apartment on the next floor. My legs, arms and back were soon aching from the effort of carrying the various things which Neville kindly handed me – chair, small pedestal tables, a chest of drawers, china, glass, records and record-player, books, the bust of Wagner, a Persian rug, an ormolu clock, and a large pile of sheets, pillow-cases and towels.

'Neville – '

'Don't waste time talking, Rasy. The monster will be here any minute.'

'I can't manage the chaise-longue by myself.'

'Let's put it in your room, then. I couldn't possibly manoeuvre it up those stairs.'

The inspector was over an hour late. Neville tested his 'Watteau smile' in the hall mirror before opening the door to him.

'Mr Packer?'

'That's how I sign myself. Mr Drake?'

'I was beginning to think you weren't coming.'

' "Think", Mr Drake? "Hope", don't you mean?'

'Not at all, Mr Packer. I'm not amused by your little witticism, I'm afraid. Necessity, rather than choice, has made me tardy in my payments. Call me old-fashioned, but unlike the majority of people today, I happen to have a social conscience.'

'An encouraging start, Mr Drake.'

'Won't you come in, Mr Packer? I'm not feeling well enough to discuss my financial embarrassments in a draught.'

'It *is* nippy, isn't it?'

'Very.'

The inspector entered, whistling tunelessly.

'Which way to Armageddon, Mr Drake?'

'To your left, Mr Packer.'

'Spartan,' said the inspector of taxes after surveying the contents of Neville's bedroom, including me. 'It's like a monk's cell. Except for those funny photographs.' He peered at Kirsten Flagstad as Brunnhilde. 'Is she your pin-up, Mr Drake?'

'In a sense, Mr Packer.'

'It takes all sorts.'

'It does indeed. This is my lodger – Mr Hugh Smart. He occupies what used to be my drawing-room, before I fell on hard times. He is a young actor whose potential brilliance has already been recognized by one of our foremost critics. It is my privilege, Mr Packer, to introduce you to the definitive Reynaldo.'

'Pleased to meet you, Mr Smart. How much rent do you pay Mr Drake, may I ask?'

'I charge him a pound a week,' Neville broke in. 'He's barely out of his teens, Mr Packer, and he hasn't worked for six months. I couldn't take more from him. You'll remember my kindness, won't you, Hugh, when you're famous?'

'Yes, of course I will, Neville.'

'Bless you. Take a seat, Mr Packer.'

'There doesn't seem to be one, Mr Drake.'

'You'll find the divan quite comfortable.'

Mr Packer sat on the bed, and opened his briefcase.

'Yes, I regard young Hugh here as an insurance policy of sorts. I may be a philanthropist, Mr Packer, but I'm not a fool. He's so obviously destined for greatness that I can't fail. I'll be rich in my old age.'

'According to our records, Mr Drake, you haven't paid us a single penny for five years.'

'As long as that, is it, Mr Packer?'

'It's as long as that, Mr Drake.'

'Are you certain?'

'Positive. Why do you live in such an expensive part of London, Mr Drake?'

'Why do you ask, Mr Packer?'

'It strikes me that if you found a cheaper place in a more modest area, you could then afford to settle your taxes and perhaps buy yourself a few sticks of furniture.'

'I'm touched by your interest in my welfare, but I have to keep up appearances. I really, really have to.'

'What type of appearances might you be referring to, Mr Drake?'

'You're playing games with me, Mr Packer. You know perfectly well.'

'I've no idea what you're talking about, Mr Drake, to put it bluntly.'

'Such is fame, Hugh. Regard Mr Packer's blunt treatment of me as an awful warning. "Où sont les neiges d'antan?" Where, indeed?'

'Fame, Mr Drake? Did I hear you correctly?'

'You did. In a small way – I must stress that: *in a small way* – I was famous once. I don't expect you to remember the films I was in more than a decade ago – '

'Films?'

'That's right,' Neville sighed.

'Then I do remember who you are. That nose – how could I forget it? You were in *They Flew to Glory*.'

'I was.'

'You played the mechanic, didn't you?'

'I did.'

'You had an accent, I think.'

'Yes.'

'Irish?'

Neville stopped beaming. 'No, Mr Packer.'

'My joke, Mr Packer. You were as Cockney as jellied eels and Rosie Lee.'

'I hope I was.'

'You were wonderful – if I may say so – Mr Drake.'

Neville looked at me as he replied: 'Thank you, Mr Packer. Over the years, I've received a lot of praise for that performance.'

'You don't surprise me. But back to business for a moment.

There doesn't seem to be anything here that I can accept in lieu of payment.'

'What about the curtains? My bed? The photographs?'

'They wouldn't, with all due respect, fetch very much.'

'Then my fate is in your hands, Mr Packer.'

'You have a fine turn of phrase, Mr Drake. You're an artist if ever I saw one, and I've had to visit a few head-in-the-clouds types since I took on this job, I can tell you. You all have one thing in common.'

'And what is that, Mr Packer?'

'A disregard for money, Mr Drake.'

'It *is* the root of all evil, isn't it?'

'I don't suppose you could send me a small amount of the evil stuff every week, could you, Mr Drake?'

'Do you mean in instalments, Mr Packer?'

'Five pounds a throw, Mr Drake?'

'It would necessitate some scrimping and saving on my part — we'll be eating margarine instead of butter from now on, Hugh — but I think I could find five pounds to send you —'

'Regularly, Mr Drake?'

'Without fail, Mr Packer.' Neville picked up the battered Bible and kissed it. 'You have my solemn promise.'

'I'd rather have it in writing, Mr Drake.'

So Mr Packer dictated a letter, which Neville wrote in his best hand. Then the two of them Packered and Draked each other for an eternity, it seemed. Every scene of *They Flew to Glory* was analysed and, eventually, praised.

'When you said — and I hope I quote exactly, Mr Drake — when you said "The bleedin' control's gorn, Guv. Lawks-a-mercy, what the deuce am I to do now, I arsk yer?" I felt my flesh go cold.'

'Powerful writing, Mr Packer. No actor worth his salt could miss the mark with lines of that calibre.'

'You mustn't belittle your achievement, Mr Drake.'

They dissected the last reel ('Such a stirring march, Mr Drake.' 'One of his finest, Mr Packer.' 'When the squadron-leader smiled at you and said "Well done, Higgins," tears were pricking at my eyes, Mr Drake.' 'Understatement, Mr Packer — it always works') and the taxman left.

'How was I?' Neville asked.

'Outrageous. Awful. You were outrageously awful. I've never seen such dire over-acting. When you kissed that Bible! He must be a fool to be taken in like that.'

'On the contrary. He's a man of rare discernment. I shall have to lie down and rest now—I'm utterly exhausted.'

'Is the monk's cell to remain frugal?'

'What a ridiculous question, Rasy. You can take your time putting everything back, but try and be quiet doing it—there's a dear.'

Neville slept while I laboured. I was contemplating cracking his skull with Wagner Smug when he woke up.

'Can we afford to drink cocoa with our bread and margarine tonight?' I asked. 'Or will it be water again?'

'Ah, the room's its old self once more. Did you work these wonders on your own, Rasy?'

'No, Neville. Some passing sprites saw me struggling and came to my assistance. They even helped me with that bloody chaise-longue.'

'You *are* good to me. I don't deserve it. I'll go and buy some champagne.'

'You're in an uncharacteristically extravagant mood, are you?'

'Yes, Sourpuss, I am. Even you have to admit that for once I have good cause to celebrate. I shan't be sent to prison, and I have a nice big cheque to spend. I shall open a new bank account tomorrow. That will be my seventh.'

'Your seventh?'

'Must you shout? Yes, Loudmouth, my seventh. I like to be in funds *somewhere*. As soon as I'm overdrawn in one, I start another. I'll get some cooked meats from the delicatessen to eat with our magnum. You've passed the friendship test today with a Beta plus.'

Two days later Neville received a letter from the tax office. Would I be an angel and scan its contents? Would I oblige with a nod if the news was bad?

'It's from Mr Packer. He writes "It was an honour meeting you, Mr Drake. I hope this finds you well. I trust you didn't sprain anything replacing the furniture. Yours in admiration, Ernest V. Packer, H.M. Inspector of Taxes". You were right, Neville. He *is* a man of rare discernment.'

The doctor's long agony ended at last.

'Trust him to go peacefully. When it's my turn, one of these fine days, I'll be screaming my head off, I can see it now.'

'He had six strokes, Mother.'

'What if he had? It's how he *went* I'm talking about. I know I shan't have the good fortune to go in my sleep.'

'I didn't realize you owned a crystal ball.'

'You can keep your sarcasm to yourself, You. All I was trying to say was that I'll be very surprised if I die as gently as he did.'

'I'm going up to look at him.'

'Whatever for?'

'To pay my respects.'

'He won't hear you, will he? You can just as well pay them at the funeral.'

'It's not the same.'

'You're even more morbid than when you were a boy.'

I hesitated before kissing Dr Cottie's cheek. What if he sprang up and struck me for my unmanly behaviour? I touched him, to test that he was really dead.

Forgetting that I had once regarded him as Claudius, I put my lips to his tight, cold skin. His eyes didn't open, as I half expected them to. If I pulled back the lids, I wondered, would I be warmed again by their defiant brightness? No, of course not. Their lustre was gone, for ever.

Impulsively, I said 'Aha!' and laughed. I was still laughing when Mother entered the Temple of Wisdom.

'It's funny, is it, You, a man lying dead? He wasn't perfect, as I know to my cost, but that's no cause for mocking him. You've a strange way of paying your respects, I must say.'

'I was remembering something he once said.'

'Some bit of man's talk, I suppose. I've yet to meet a man without a dirty mind. Don't bother to soil *my* ears with it.'

'I'm sure the doctor was always clean in word and deed.'

'Then you can't be sure of much, and that's a truth. Cover him up, will you? I'll bet a nickel to a brass farthing you won't stare at me like that when I'm laid out. Cover him up. Come downstairs where it's warm. Cover him up and let him be.'

'F. Leonard Cottie has been whisked off to the eternal consulting room, I see.'

'Is there an obituary in *The Times* then?'

'If you can call "The noted physician and surgeon, F. Leonard Cottie, has died at his home in London at the age of ninety-three" an obituary, the answer is yes. Did you know he was dead?'

'Mother rang with the news yesterday evening.'

'You might have told me.'

'I didn't wish to interrupt the performance of *Parsifal.*'

'I should like to have met him, as you were well aware. I shall never meet him now.'

'True.'

'I asked you on several occasions to effect an introduction.'

'That was one of *his* expressions. And I told *you* on several occasions that he was very, very ill.'

'And I observed on several occasions that you appeared to be afraid that the mere sight of me would kill him off.'

I'd been afraid of something else: Neville's mockery. Deprived of speech, the doctor had spoken eloquently: 'Look,' he'd said, 'I live.' He'd ceased to be the author of *With Stethoscope and Scalpel.*

'Did you say he was ninety-three?'

'No. *The Times* does.'

'That means he was in his eighties when he and Mother; when he and Mrs Parkes … '

'Mrs Parkes?'

'Mrs Parkes. She was a force of nature. She served us tea. She's in prison.'

'What did they have in common—your mother and this forceful criminal?'

'Nothing much.'

'You are being annoyingly enigmatic, Rasy.'

'The doctor made love to them. Mother dubbed him "the old stoat". When she first agreed to satisfy his requirements, she never imagined they would be quite so athletic. He used to make a whooping noise, like a Red Indian, during their sessions.'

'Light is dawning. Now perhaps you'll tell me why this Mrs Parkes is doing time.'

'She kept a brothel in Putney.'

'That's where tea was served, was it?'

'And home-made scones.'

'You went there with F. Leonard?'

'Yes.'

'F. Leonard took you?'

'Yes.'

'What for?'

'What do you think? Why does one usually go to a brothel?'

'Not for tea and scones.'

'No, Neville, not for tea and scones. They were extra.'

'Am I to understand that you went there for the obvious purpose?'

'Yes, you are.'

'You, of all people?'

'Me, of all people.'

'How old were you?'

'I was sixteen exactly.'

'And a virgin?'

'On arrival. Things were different at ten past five. Correction: one particular thing was different at ten past five. Need I be more explicit?'

'My God, you're a secretive bastard. You go about with the air of someone who should be tossing off epistles to the Corinthians, and here you are admitting that you once had a fuck. You could at least blush.'

'Oh more than once, Neville, more than once. I apologize for my saintly demeanour, and my secretive nature. I apologize, too, for not boring you to a state verging on the comatose with the details of my sexual prowess. But, most of all, I apologize for not inserting my dick to the deafening accompaniment of the Prize Song — oh please, please accept my apologies for not doing that!'

'Bravo! Bravissimo! Lose your temper, Rasy. Pitch your voice just a fraction higher, and let rip.'

'No.'

'Spoilsport. I've been longing for you to erupt. Give me an encore, Rasy. It's inconsiderate of you to keep all that splendid venom to yourself.'

Fred and Adele Astaire, Winston Churchill, Noël Coward, Alexander Fleming, Greta Garbo, the Aga Khan, Pablo Picasso, Albert Schweitzer and Jan Sibelius were unable to attend the funeral of F. Leonard Cottie, M.D., F.R.C.S.

I was present, though, and so was Mother. Neville was there, too. So was a woman who either glowered at us or wept.

'He never told me about you,' she said to Mother after the ceremony. 'And with good reason.'

'Whoever you are, I can't recall him ever mentioning you.'

'He always fancied himself as the Casanova type. He used to say he could have married any woman he wanted — film stars, duchesses, the crême de la crême. But he got you instead. I'm not surprised he never boasted of it.'

Mother was purple with fury. The woman prodded me in the ribs with her umbrella and asked 'Is this your son?'

'He is.'

'Is he your son, or isn't he?'

'Yes!' shouted Mother.

'I thought you'd admit it in the end. I had an idea there was another liaison going on. That's why he never had any money to blow on me — he was keeping you and your skinny offspring in the lap of luxury. Set you up in a fine house, I suppose, and gave you every comfort. You both look as if you're accustomed to the best of everything. When I think of all the nights he came home late to a ruined dinner! Now I know why he never complained — he'd been eating and guzzling with you.'

I was the recipient of more prods.

'Is he legitimate?'

'Is he *what*?'

'Is he legitimate, or isn't he?'

'Of course he is!'

'Are you saying yes?'

'Yes!'

'I've spent thirty years of my life playing second fiddle to a bigamist. This outfit I'm wearing to mourn him in cost me a small fortune—the shoes alone are worth more than anything on *your* back.'

To my surprise, Mother ignored this insult. She said firmly: 'I didn't marry him. He was a snob. He only wanted a skivvy.'

'Are you talking to me?'

We realized then that the woman was slightly deaf.

'I—did—not—marry—him.'

'You didn't?'

'No.'

'You said *he* was legitimate.'

I was prodded again.

'He—is.'

'He can't be.'

'He—is—the—son—of—another—man.'

'You shameless creature! You were my husband's bit of fluff, were you? You were his kept woman?'

Mother smiled. 'He did say once that I put all other women in the shade.'

'You were his fancy piece? You were his mistress?'

'I was.'

'You're not exactly glamorous.'

'Neither are you.'

Mother tried to look sympathetic while the woman blubbered.

'Oh Edwin! Edwin!'

'Edwin?'

'Edwin! Edwin!'

'Who—is—Edwin?'

'You should know. You saw him often enough.'

'No — one — named — Edwin — has — ever — crossed — my

—path.'

'A likely story. Who do you imagine was in that coffin?'

'Dr—Cottie. Leonard. *F.* Leonard.'

The vicar, who had been standing rigid with embarrassment throughout the confrontation, stepped forward, took an audible breath, and asked the woman in a piercingly loud voice if by any chance she was the widow of Mr Edwin Lyons.

'I am. I am.'

'Oh dear. How very unfortunate. You—have—attended—the —wrong—service. The—service—for—poor—Mr—Lyons—is— next—in—chapel.'

'Next? You mean that wasn't? Is that what you mean? Do you mean that was someone else?'

'Yes, Mrs Lyons.'

'Edwin's is to come?'

'Yes, Mrs Lyons.'

'Dear Edwin. I'm so pleased. Dear Edwin. I called him Teddy Bear, you know. I'm so relieved. He would most certainly not have associated with a woman of her kind. I shall kneel down and pray for him until these—' she looked at Mother, at Neville, at me '—people have left.' She walked purposefully away from us, down the aisle. 'Dear Edwin, of course you were always at your club. Of course you were. You loved your snooker.'

'Well,' said Mother. 'Well!'

She had more to say in the car taking us back to The Elms: 'She couldn't hide it from me.'

'Who couldn't hide what, Mother?'

'That dreaful Edwin woman—she may have fooled you two with her la-di-da tones, but not me. I'd stake my life on it she comes from beyond Doncaster. Southerners have their faults, like all of us, but they don't behave as heathens do, as she did.'

'I thought you showed great patience and tact, Mrs Smart,' said Neville.

'If I'd stooped to her level, Mr Drake, all hell would have broken loose.'

*

Not aspirin; not gas; no more nonsense with rope—a stranger, hired to scour the Thames, would heave my carcass into his boat with the other debris.

A jump would do it. It was as easy as falling off a parapet.

In a calm state of mind, on a calm spring night, I made my way towards the river.

The Bridge at Midnight

'To my astonishment'; 'to my surprise' — this past month, attempting to bring the dead to life, I've been surprised and astonished. Keeping the company of my resurrected mother has given me an unexpected pleasure; a pleasure I never experienced while she was living. I had taken her uniqueness for granted. Today, I almost wish I could celebrate her malevolent spirit.

There can be no 'almost' about my regard for the doctor. Nothing less than total, undying admiration is due to a man who could write:

> I well recall (ah, what a blessed gift is Memory!) encountering that historic figure, the Mahatma Gandhi, as he strolled in the somewhat tepid mid-day sun along that famed highway Whitehall. I was at that time a humble medic, and he was — here the grateful memorist must apologize to the gentle reader for a little inappropriate but alas, irresistible, levity — in a state I fear I must call PRE-historic. Yes, his great deeds were yet to be done!
>
> With his brown skin, spotless loin-cloth, sandals and spectacles he looked a Typical Indian. As he made his dignified way towards me, I was struck by a quality I can only describe as Magnetic. No words had been said, but his presence Told All. (It is a quality, by the by, I have detected in other great men. There are those — it has recently been brought to my attention — who have noted it in myself. Of that, however, Basta!) His eyes, even behind glass, were deep pools of Wisdom. I was drawn to them against my will for, truth to tell, my first hernia was, on that never-to-be-forgotten day, playing havoc with my thoughts. Would I succeed, or wouldn't I? Would I add lustre to the pro-

fession that Sir William Harvey and Sir Thomas Browne, those renowned ancients, had graced so luminously in the dark days of Medicine? Would I, or would I not, pull through?

I raised my hat to the diminutive Indian (measure not a man's abilities by his physical stature — Wolfgang Amadeus Mozart, whose melodies enchant us yet, was small; yea, mighty Napoleon was hardly more than a midget) and bade him good morning.

A disarming smile appeared on the future prophet's features, for at the very moment that I addressed him Big Ben struck the hour. It was now twelve of the clock.

'Good afternoon,' he corrected me.

Despite my mental anxiety, I could not but smile myself at this display of wit.

I stared at his retreating figure until it disappeared from view. Observing his stately progress, I said to myself (I probably, such was the impression he had made upon me, spoke the words aloud) 'There goes a Man of Destiny if ever I saw one.' I do not think that History has proved me incorrect.

I turned on my heel and hurried to the hospital. I was never to see Gandhi in the flesh again.

In the Temple of Wisdom, impatiently craving the white-hot inspiration that refused to take possession of me, I'd dreamed of a glorious future. Ten years later, in the room once occupied by the creator of *Corporeal Cantatas*, I calmly examined my humdrum present.

What, at twenty-five, had I achieved? None of my grand ambitions had been fulfilled. At my age, Mozart — 'whose melodies' etc. — had written ... oh, just think of what he'd written! Those works of genius — the poems, plays, novels, essays that would one day make up the Standard Edition of my writings — where were they? Inside my thick skull was the simple answer. They seemed quite content to make that their resting place.

And the Edmund Kean *de nos jours* — how was he progressing? Not too well, when you thought about it. Was he scaling the highest reaches of his art? Not really. Since his definitive Reynaldo he had played Terry, a moronic plumber's mate, in a television play entitled *Grit in the Ballcock*, and the tragic Marcus Sutcliffe in *Murder in Mayfair* ('You must understand, Inspector, that I wasn't the only man Antonia drove to madness. She knew, damn her, how to enthrall and enchant. I've done the world a service by killing her.') Perhaps he was doing the world a service, too, by not offering it his Hamlet, Lear and Coriolanus.

I decided not to say goodbye to Neville. He had worries of his own. Kundry was bathing his wounds as I left.

I looked down at the gently flowing Thames. Yes. I would do it now. No one was around: a quick jump; a splash; then I'd be nothing. I was poised to climb on to the parapet when I looked up and saw a young woman on the bridge near by. I called to her. 'Wait!' I shouted. 'Stop!'

I went out to die that night. I saved a life instead.

'What are you doing?'
'What does it look like?'
'I don't think you should.'
'I didn't ask for your opinion.'
'I'm giving it, nevertheless.'
'Go away, will you?'
'No.'
'Just pretend you never saw me.'
'You mustn't do it.'
'Why?'
'Because it's wrong.'
'Are you a Catholic?'
'No.'
'Then don't talk shit.'
'I'm talking sense. Please get down.'
'Sod you, you interfering bastard. Go away.'
'Tell me what's the matter. Come to my flat. Tell me what's wrong over a drink.'
'The only thing I want to tell you is to fuck off.'
'I'll listen to you. I'll help you, I promise.'
'Are you mad?'
'I could be. Come down.'

'I don't need your help. I've nothing to say. You can give me a push if you like. That would be helping.'

I moved towards her. I grabbed her waist, and pulled her to the ground. We struggled. She got to her feet and kicked me in the crotch. I screamed.

'Serves you right. Have I hurt you?'

'No.'

'Of course I have. I meant to. Your wife won't be happy if I've put you out of action.'

She had the effrontery to laugh.

'I'm not married.'

I doubled up with pain.

'I'm sorry,' she said. 'You annoyed me. Take my arm. Do you live in this area?'

'No. It's quite a walk from here.'

'Have you enough money for a taxi?'

It occurred to me that I would have been good pickings for whoever found me in the river: I had twenty pounds in my wallet.

'Have you enough money? Because I haven't.'

'Yes.'

'Does your invitation still stand?'

'Which invitation?'

'If I climb up there again, will you remember? "Come to my flat," you said. You said I could tell you about my troubles over a drink. You probably didn't mean it.'

'Of course I did.'

'I like vodka best. It must be my Russian blood.'

'Your Russian blood?'

'Yes, I'm half Russian. I can see you don't believe me, but I am.'

'What's your name?'

'Natasha. Natasha O'Connor.'

'There's only brandy, Miss O'Connor.'

'That'll do, I suppose.'

'It's more medicinal than vodka.'

'I'm not worried about my health. I spent most of my childhood in hospital – diphtheria first, then rheumatic fever. I saw more of nurses and doctors than I did of my parents.'

'How very sad.'

'It wasn't sad at all. I enjoyed being waited on. I don't need your pity.'

'I simply said –'

'I'm sick of people pitying me. Why the hell should they? Pass me the drink, and stop looking considerate.'

'Here you are.'

'I ought to throw it in your face. How are your balls?'

'Safe and sound.'

'I'm in no way grateful to you. I hope you understand that.'

'You've made your feelings very clear.'

'Just as long as you realize that this particular damsel in distress resents the intrusion of her knight in shining armour. You have lots of possessions.'

'Not really.'

'Compared to me you have. I find this room stifling. I want to break everything in it, especially the ornaments. I hate people who surround themselves with silly bits of china. What's that music?'

'Wagner.'

'And who's playing it?'

'The man I share this flat with.'

'Is he a fool like you?'

'Oh no, he's quite different.'

'I'm glad to hear it. One of you's enough. I wish I'd met him tonight instead. He might have given me a push. My glass is empty."

As I filled it she said 'It's because I'm used to drinking vodka. I throw my head back, Russian style, and let it slide down.'

'You shouldn't do that with brandy.'

'I know, Saviour, I know. I'm well aware of all the things I shouldn't do. If you're going to seduce me, then it's better that I'm drunk.'

'I have no intention of seducing you. No intention whatsoever.'

'Haven't you?'

'No.'

'That makes a change. In spite of the fact that I'm not beautiful

—and don't you dare tell me I am, you lying creep, don't you bloody dare—men seem to want to sleep with me. I think I must look disposable. You take her, and you leave her. I was raped, by the way, when I was fourteen.'

'Were you?'

'Yes, I was. Very nastily. Twice. At Kew.'

'Not in the gardens?'

'Where else?'

'Well, the—'

'I was a schoolgirl one minute and a woman of the world the next. He had a goatee beard and wore a monocle. He pushed me behind a eucalyptus. I bled like anything.'

I was too shocked to express sympathy.

'When he'd finished, a Chinaman took over. He chewed tobacco while he was doing it. I pulled his pigtail, and he slapped me hard across the face. Then the two of them ran off. I tried to scream, but couldn't. I stood there, shaking, in a pool of blood.'

'You poor soul.'

'I had to be aborted, naturally. You're a lousy barman. I'll help myself. It's quicker.'

'Rasy, there seems to be a woman in the bathroom.'

'Not *seems*, Neville. There *is*.'

'I caught a glimpse of her. Backing away from the uncomely spectacle, I noted that she isn't exactly Rubensesque. I've seen boys with bigger tits. If you've screwed her, I beg of you not to have the temerity to admit it.'

'She had the bed to herself. I slept on the floor.'

'Is she an old friend?'

'No. I met her last night.'

'You were drunk, of course?'

'I was sober.'

'Where did you meet her?'

'On Lambeth bridge.'

'And what were you doing on Lambeth bridge?'

'Admiring the Thames.'

'Was she admiring it as well?'

'In her fashion.'

'Rasy dear, do be careful. You won't heed my warning, but I'm telling you just the same.' He reverted to French as Natasha, wearing my dressing-gown, came into the room, her wet feet making a squelching sound on the carpet: 'Elle est dangereuse.'

'Neville, this is Natasha.'

'Pleased to meet you,' said Neville curtly.

'You're obviously not.'

'No, I can't say I am.'

'But you did. A moment ago you said you were pleased to meet me. You're a liar, aren't you?'

'Are you usually so charming, or is today a special occasion? What lovely company you keep, Mr Smart. You must introduce me to more of your friends. Meanwhile, with great reluctance, I shall deny myself further delightful converse with the fascinating young person who is currently engaged in transforming a Persian rug into a dish-cloth.'

He blew her a kiss, and exited, closing the door with studied quietness.

'That's somebody else who doesn't like me. I'm not worried.'

'If you're not worried, why are you crying?'

'I wish you'd left me alone. I wish you'd walked past. I wish I wasn't here, or anywhere. This time yesterday I was telling myself I would be dead this time today.'

'Get dressed.'

'I told you a lie last night.'

'About the rape?'

'That was true!' she shouted. 'In every sordid detail. No, it's my name. I'm not half Russian and I'm not Natasha. I'm called Nancy.'

'Nancy O'Connor.'

'Why O'Connor?'

'You said your surname was O'Connor.'

'Well, it's not. It's Williams, for your information.'

'Thank you. Let me introduce myself. I'm Peter Smart. I do have other names, but that's my real one.'

★

145

I put the Persian rug out to dry on the balcony. The sun warmed me as well. I felt renewed, refreshed. I was alive, and so was Nancy Williams, or Natasha O'Connor, or whatever she chose to call herself in future.

Weeks passed, and I came to believe that Nancy had no future. I neither saw nor heard from her. The Thames's scourer, I decided, had fished her out; had dumped her in his boat; had reaped his reward.

I learned, soon enough, that he hadn't.

Between Natasha on the bridge and Nancy in my life there was a lull. Things happened: the doctor's will was read, and Mother came to dinner.

I went with Mother to the office of Messrs Crisp & Vereker, Solicitors, Lincoln's Inn Fields. Mr Crisp gave us tea and biscuits; Mr Vereker told us he would read the will.

'I'm afraid it's a trifle long-winded.'

'Only a trifle, Mr Vereker?'

'Well, no, Mrs Smart, it's a good deal more than a trifle.'

'I had an idea it might be.'

'I'll do my best to make short work of it.'

We settled ourselves to listen.

'Dr Cottie's last will and testament begins somewhat unconventionally with a few words of advice to me. "Read it in a joyful manner, Mr Vereker," he writes. "Employ your vocal skills to the utmost. I myself shall be listening with my fellow shades and appraising your performance. *Con brio,* Mr Vereker; not to say *allegro vivace.*" '

'He had some funny ways.'

'He liked his little joke, Mrs Smart.'

'He never made *me* laugh.'

'His was a quirky sense of humour.'

'His was.'

We heard, through a bemused solicitor, the doctor's thoughts on mortality. Death, we learned, is the end of life. It is not to be feared. It is to be accepted. It is, in certain circumstances, to be welcomed. Without the knowledge of its existence (or non-existence), what would Life be? A bauble. Are Life and Death showy trinkets? They are not.

'Does he mention money?'

'Yes, Mrs Smart. Eventually.'

'I was only wondering. I was brought up to believe that wills had to do with worldly goods. This one sounds more like a sermon.'

'You will, I assure you, hear something to your benefit.'

'I was only wondering, Mr Vereker.'

'You have good reason to wonder. Where had I got to?'

' "They are not".'

'Thank you, Mr Smart. "They are not. Life, then, is not a plaything. My own modest existence should stand as a shining exemplar to those bent on the fleshly pleasures ... " '

'The *what?*'

' "The fleshly pleasures." '

'That's what I thought I heard you say. Well, Mr Vereker, you take it from me that the doctor didn't use his bedroom for talking about life and death and all the other highfalutin nonsense in. Oh no. Until that first stroke put an end to his goings-on, he was like a stoat when he was in the mood. I've known him on occasions finish one minute, catch his breath back, and start again the next. He wasn't a saint, Mr Vereker, believe you me.'

'I'm sure you're right.'

'I am. A stoat hasn't a mind to see what he's doing, but the doctor had.'

The solicitor looked confused. 'No,' he said, 'the stoat is not the most astute of creatures. Shall I soldier on?'

'The sooner we hear the worst the better.'

A brief résumé of Dr Cottie's long life came next: he was born; he attended – sometimes unwillingly – a famed academy; he became a humble medic after hearing Sir Royston Hammond (of Fond Memory) lecture on disorders of the cranium ...

I smiled, but Mother fumed and fidgeted. 'Listen to it,' she said, under her breath. 'Was there ever such an old fool?'

'We have at last arrived – you'll be relieved to hear, Mrs Smart – at the subject of money.'

'I should hope so.'

There were four beneficiaries: Mother ('To my smilingly solicitous housekeeper, Mrs Ellen Smart—a Nell if ever I saw one—the sum of £20,000, and the possession of that property, The Elms, in which she gratified my every whim'); Dame Ada Keen ('last heard of in the vicinity of Nottingham'), to whom the doctor bequeathed the royalties for his autobiography; Dobbin's Rest Farm ('The aged members of the noble family *equus caballus* are never far from my thoughts. To Farmer Gilchrist, devoted protector of the solid-hoofed perissodactyl quadruped, I leave sufficient moneys for the purchase of hay— £100,000'), and myself. The 'more than promising young Thespian' received £10,000.

'That's it,' said Mr Vereker, casting the will aside with a look of relief. 'I hope I read it to the doctor's satisfaction.'

'Perhaps Mr Smart would care to give an actor's opinion of your performance,' said Mr Crisp.

'It was most impressive.'

'Thank you. Everything's nicely settled, is it?'

'Very nicely, Mr Vereker,' I replied.

'I take it you're pleased as well, Mrs Smart?'

'I'd be more pleased if I knew why he left so much money to that "noble family" with the daft name. What, I want to know, do they need hay for? I mean to say, with the amount he's passed on to them they could well afford mattresses.'

'The *equus caballus* is a horse.'

'A horse?'

'Yes. And Dobbin's Rest Farm is a kind of home, or hospice, for old horses.'

'When I was young, horses past their prime went to the knacker's yard to be cut up for the benefit of dogs and cats. I don't wish to sound ungrateful, but I think I deserve more respect than an animal. I've nothing against horses—I got through *Black Beauty* as a girl.'

'Think of it this way, Mrs Smart—there are many of *them*, but only one of *you*. The doctor has not been ungenerous.'

We said goodbye to the solicitors, and made our way down the stairs. Outside, in the dying light, Mother suddenly exploded:

'Horses! It isn't the money, it's the principle. He'd have walked down the street with a horse, but not with me.'

'You're rich now, Mother. You have The Elms too.'

'And you're not exactly poor, are you, You? I suppose you'll go to pieces and spend the lot on women or worse, like those playboys in dark glasses you see in the papers.'

'I'm sure I shan't.'

'I should hope not.'

'I'll take you to the bus stop.'

'No, you won't. I'm coming with you. Your friend Mr Drake has invited me to dinner tonight, which is something you've never done. You can call us a taxi, now you're a man of means.'

'Neville said nothing to me about it.'

'I'll be on my best behaviour. I shan't disgrace you.'

In the cab, I asked Mother if the doctor had ever mentioned Dame Ada Keen.

'No, not that I recall. I wonder what she did for him. I suppose I'm ignorant, but I couldn't make out what it was he left to her.'

'His royalties.'

'The only royalties I've heard of live in palaces.'

'They're earnings, Mother. The money he made from his book.'

Mother's face brightened. A smile that wasn't quite a smile was followed by a laugh that wasn't quite a laugh.

'I'm glad I'm not in her shoes. If she *has* a pair. Earnings! I saw him give the postman a copy once.'

She continued not quite laughing until we reached Paddington.

'I hope you haven't cooked any of that fancy foreign muck,' were her first words to Neville.

'Are you a wealthy woman now, Mrs Smart?'

'There are horses who are wealthier, and that's a truth. They'll be swishing their tails with joy tonight, I'll be bound.'

I translated for Neville's benefit. I told him Mother had little cause for complaint, and that I, too, had reason to be grateful to the doctor.

'We must celebrate. We must toast your good fortune in champagne. I was feeling extravagant this afternoon, and bought some.'

149

'Mother won't drink it, Neville.'

'Yes, Mother will,' Mother snapped. 'Mother certainly will. Mother feels the need this once, Mother does. Mother will accept a glass with pleasure.'

'Give me your coat, Mrs Smart. Make yourself comfortable.'

Mother drank champagne. Later, with her *Coquilles St Jacques à la Provençale,* she drank Gewurtztraminer. Then, with her *Boeuf à la Gardiane,* she drank Medoc. When Neville brought in the cheese, she scorned Cheddar and chose Brie. With her *Compôte d'Abricots* she drank Yquem. She did not refuse brandy after dinner. She drank everything Neville offered her—to my surprise, to his delight. Alcohol neither mellowed nor saddened her, though food had its usual effect.

'I have a funny system,' she explained between coughs. 'If I eat a lot, my throat is sure to suffer.'

At three in the morning she announced abruptly that she had better be making tracks. 'You can wake my host up, You, and tell him I'm going.'

I nudged Neville's shoulder. His eyes opened, and closed. They opened again. He stared at Mother in bewilderment. He smiled. 'I wasn't asleep, Mrs Smart.'

'I should hope you were. It's no compliment to a lady for a man to snore when he isn't even asleep. I was just saying to him here that I must be on my way.'

'Oh, must you?'

'Yes, I must. I enjoyed my meal, Mr Drake. I didn't expect to, but I did. I'd have enjoyed a plain steak and kidney pudding and an apple pie even more, but there, you can't have everything. You can hail me a taxi, You. A woman isn't safe walking the streets of London at this time of night.'

'It's been a pleasure entertaining you,' said Neville.

'Has it? Well, if you say so, I suppose it has. When you come to sit at my table, Mr Drake, you'll know what it is you're putting into your mouth. I don't go in for disguise at The Elms. In my kitchen beef's beef, a shrimp's a shrimp, and good English vegetables are cooked in water fresh from the tap. There's a lesson in that, for those who care to find it.'

Mother had a message for the taxi driver, too. After I'd told him where to take her, she added: 'If you see a horse, run it over.'

I was too tired to translate. I staggered back to the flat.

'Now I know why you're as assertive as a mouse, Rasy. You had too much competition as a child. Had I been her son, I'd have murdered her—very horribly—a long time ago. I'd have chopped her into little pieces, and stuffed them in a suitcase.'

'She warmed to you.'

'That was warmth, was it?'

'As near to it as she can manage.'

'Don't think I'm not impressed, because I am. I thought she was odd at the doctor's funeral, but the word's inadequate to describe her. You and I are odd, in our different ways. She exists on a higher plane altogether. If you put her in a book—as they say—no one would believe her. We've grown accustomed to having the so-called real world writ small. Her meanness of spirit is on a scale we can no longer reckon with. Only Wagner could do her justice.'

I pictured Mother in armour, on an ailing carthorse, and laughed.

'Am I speaking to Peter, or the other one?'

'You're speaking to Peter.'

'It's Nancy.'

'I recognized your voice.'

'I don't suppose you want to speak to me, do you? I'll ring off.'

'I'd given you up for dead.'

'Thanks a lot.'

'Are you free tonight?'

'Of course I am.'

'Eat with me then.'

'You don't have to invite me. I only rang up to ask if your balls were back to normal.'

'I haven't thought about them, so they must be.'

'You don't *have* to invite me, you know.'

'I'll expect you at eight.'

She arrived at seven, flustered. 'I'll sit in the lav for an hour, if you like. I got fed up with wandering around, that's why I'm early. I'll keep out of your way. Shall I wait on the stairs until you're ready?'

'No. Please come in.'

'You didn't *have* to invite me. If my company bores you stiff, it won't be my fault.'

'Do come in. I have a nice surprise for you.'

'What is it?'

'Some very superior Polish vodka.'

'I've never drunk it.'

'Not even Russian style? With your head back?'

'When I say I've never drunk it, I mean I've never drunk it.'

'Why was I under the impression that you had?'

'I've no idea.'

'I must be confusing you with someone else.'

'There can't be two of me. One's enough.'

'It so happens,' I said, steering Nancy towards my room, 'that I've never drunk vodka either. We can have a joint initiation.'

'You do sound pompous. "A joint initiation." Is *he* here?'

'Neville?'

'I don't remember his name. All I remember is the way he looked at me that morning. He would have pushed me off the bridge. He'd have laughed as he did it.'

'He's in Manchester.'

She sat on my bed. 'I'd like to sleep here again. With you.'

'No, you wouldn't.'

'Yes, I should. With you, Peter. With you holding me.'

'Here's your first vodka, Nancy.'

'I'm in love with you.'

'No, you're not. You can't be. You don't know me well enough.'

'Yes, I do.'

'You aren't drinking it like a Russian.'

'Why the hell should I? I'm English.'

'I've made a casserole.'

'I don't care what I eat, as long as it fills the empty space. I love you, I tell you.'

'Let's have another drink before dinner.'

Why had I made love to her? Why had I *twice* made love to her?

There had to be a reason, and it wasn't lust. Her flesh was too white, and her hair too red: the colours seemed to be fighting each other for dominance. Snow and flame were permanent enemies, violently opposed.

Even in the sleep following sex—how she'd clawed me; how she'd moaned; how she'd wept—her body looked restless. Even in sleep her hands needed to be fists.

I stared at Nancy and wondered about myself. The longer I stared, the more I wondered. Yes, I told myself sadly, I was repelled by her. I wasn't flattered by her protestations of love.

Then, as I stared, I realized that I felt disgust with myself for feeling repelled by a girl so obviously desperate, so fiercely unhappy.

I kissed her, by way of apology.

Oh why was I making love to her for the third time?

Neville laughed at first. 'Marriage, Rasy? You?'

'She's pregnant.'

'Tell her to take a scalding hot bath, jump down a flight of stairs and knock back a bottle of gin. If that doesn't do the trick, a sinister old lady with a button-hook shouldn't be too hard to find.'

'I shall marry her.'

'Say it again and you'll convince yourself.'

'I'm going to marry her.'

'Rasy, no.'

'Neville, yes.'

'Such conviction! Such absurd firmness of purpose! We'll discuss this matter over a magnum of the usual when I get back from the bank. *Banks*, actually. I'm closing one account in one, and opening another in another – if you'll forgive the felicitous English. I hope to find you sane on my return.'

As soon as he had gone, I phoned Mother.

'It's you, is it, You? I was just examining my crow's feet in the mirror. Why are you ringing me up?'

'I have some news for you.'

'War hasn't broken out again, has it?'

'Mother, I think I'm going to get married.'

'You?'

'Yes, Mother. Me.'

'Not you, You?'

'Yes.'

'Why do you only think? Is there something wrong with her?'

'No.'

'You'd better show her to me. You won't need my opinion, but I ought to see her. I've got cream on my fingers to dab on my face, so if you've nothing else to tell me, I'd be obliged if you rang off.'

I left her to her wrinkles ('I've more lines than a railway junction'), and thought about my life with Neville. I was tired of his arrogance, sick of his frivolousness, bored by his chatter. Most of all, I hated his pettiness.

One morning, I remembered, I was listening to a record of a Bach cantata, when he shouted from the bathroom: 'What is that sanctimonious piss you're playing?'

I didn't reply. He stormed into my room, brandishing a razor, shaving soap on his face.

'It's called *Ich habe genug*,' I said.

'I'd gathered. Would you mind turning it down? I've had enough of him assuring me that he has enough, ad nauseam. Bach really is beyond the pale.'

'Is he?'

'He's all head, dear. Totally cerebral. There's no cock in his music. And don't tell me he fathered several children –'

'I shan't.'

'– because I know. All of them bloody prodigies. I like to think there was one, just one, who incurred Dad's wrath for being tone deaf. The poor sod has my sympathy.'

I increased the volume. Minutes later, Bach was outblasted by Wagner.

I remembered, too, the aftermath of a visit to the opera.

'You're not giggling, are you?'

'Yes, Neville, I am.'

'People are glaring at you, with good reason. Please control yourself until we're out of the building.'

'Yes, Neville.'

'Cover your mouth, for Christ's sake. You can explain your perverse behaviour in the restaurant.'

The restaurant was Italian, and fashionable. The titled and famous brayed for service and received it. We didn't, despite Neville's efforts. The waiters had guessed that he was an upstart.

'How long have we been sitting here?'

'Twenty minutes.'

'I will *not* be ignored by wops. Cameriere!'

A waiter shrugged as he passed our table.

'Cameriere!'

Neville's fifth call met with a response.

'Si, signore?'

'I want drink. I want food. So does my friend.'

The waiter yawned. 'Mi dispiace, signore. Non ho capito.'

'What's he saying, Rasy?'

'He doesn't understand you.'

'Isn't it typical? Isn't it monstrous? I'm too tired and too hungry to complain. Do you speak his language?'

'A bit.'

'Speak to him—will you?—before I faint away.'

'Noi vogliamo bere e mangiare.'

'Si, signore. Subito. Lei vuole ordinare?'

The waiter handed me the menu.

'Kindly inform the greasy dago that in view of the fact that I have a civilized detestation of his country's cuisine, I require a fillet steak grilled medium to rare, a green salad with a French dressing, and some non-wop wine. Beaujolais will do.'

I ordered.

'Grazie, signore.' The waiter pointed at Neville and said to me: 'Non mi piace suo amico. E un finocchio.'

'Davvero.'

'What are you talking about?'

'Life.'

The waiter leered at me, yawned again, and left.

'What does "finocchio" mean?'

'Fennel.'

'That's a plant. How am I a plant?'

'I don't know.'

'If you don't know, why did you smile?'

'I was humouring him.'

'You are lying, Rasy, with your customary lack of expertise. Perhaps you'll answer another question truthfully. What was it about tonight's performance of *Siegfried* that amused you so?'

'His legs.'

'Whose legs?'

'Siegfried's. I mean the tenor's. I mean Frederic Jensen's.'

'I didn't notice them. But then *I* was concentrating on the music. Personally, I thought he was in glorious voice.'

'It was his varicose veins. And the piece of cotton-wool stuck on his knee. And the way he walked—hobbled rather—in those gold sandals with lifts. And that awful blond wig, complete with kiss-curls—'

'I was, as I say, concentrating on the music.'

'Neville, he did look like a plump schoolgirl—you have to admit—in his little white pleated skirt. I kept thinking his sword was a hockey stick. And as for the roguish glances he was throwing everyone! When he and Brünnhilde gave each other the come-hither, I couldn't control myself any longer.'

'So I, and a thousand others, noticed. I may be a finocchio, whatever that is, but I am not a philistine.'

'I'm sorry, Neville, but—'

'Do shut up.'

After the meal, which we ate in silence, Neville said, 'I intend travelling home alone. I find myself unable to endure your asinine company. You may speak to me again when you're a full-fledged adult.'

Then Nancy rang, and we fixed the wedding-day.

*

'You seem a sensible girl.'

'I hope my head's screwed on, Mrs Smart.'

'You look a person straight in the eye, which is always a good sign. What made you pick him?'

'Love.'

'Oh, well, I shouldn't count on that to last, if I were you. It does in books, but books aren't life, are they? If they were, I'd never read them. You keep him in hand, Nancy. You make sure he stays on the earth. He's inclined to leave it, in my experience. I was brought up to believe that that's where men and women belong, not up in the clouds. God's there; we're here—that's my view.'

'I think you're a very handsome woman, Mrs Smart.'

'If anyone else had said that, I'd have sworn they were trying to butter me up. I can take flattery from a woman. Handsome, eh? I wasn't pretty when I was young: I left prettiness to them that had it. You're not pretty either, but you've got character. You'll turn out handsome, too, but you'll have to cope with liver spots and crow's feet, and that's a truth. Do you approve of what he does for a living?'

'Peter?'

'You're not marrying the cat.'

'I haven't seen him act.'

'You have a treat in store. Hasn't she, You? Oh, you should see him cavort! I saw him do Macbeth's wife when he was a boy, with a green dress on, and red hair similar to yours, and a knife with blood on it.'

'I've played a lot of parts since then, Mother.'

'More's the pity.'

Shortly before my marriage, I received a strange letter. It reached me via The Elms. Mother had scribbled on the envelope: *It looks as if it's from your aunt on his side who gave herself the name of Mosford.*

It wasn't.

Dear Peter or Pete as we use to call you —
*This letter is from your old pal Mrs Long — but because I can't
read or write and only ever could put a X — I am arsking Mr
Burgess who your Granny use to call Edna and then it caught on
and we all did — He is writeing it down as I say it out loud — It is
sad news Pete so bear your self your Auntie Hilda past on last
Friday the funerall is on Wednesday if you are not busy you
ought to get here by TWO O CLOCK which is when it happens — You have had your life to lead which is why we haven't
seen you so if you are to busy to come and we can't talk to you
like in the old days I better tell you that your Auntie went a bit
funny — She was allways a bit but not so much as she went — She
use to cry at weddings but she did only more so till the vicar
called her a nuisence and she stoped — Then she locked her self in
your Grannys house and we had to break the door in you could
smell it from the street — She and water werent pals the day we
broke in — She was crying her heart out Pete and it turned mine
over to hear her and the only word on her lips was Edward — After
all this time it struck us dumb — It was pityfull — She died on Friday
in the hospital — You will be a ornament at the funerall I saw you
as a plummer on the tele vision you were good as a plummer —
Yours truly Mrs Long — Minnie to you.
P.S. There will be a Spread and Drink in The Wheatsheaf
after Pete — 'Edna'.*

It was Thursday. Aunt Hilda had been in the earth a few
hours only. I hadn't thought of her for years.

She had cried out for Edward. My father had cried out for
Alice. Silence, then darkness, had answered them.

'Are you Mr Williams? Nancy's father?'

'I am, if it's any business of yours. What's happened to her
now? She hasn't tried to do herself in again, has she?'

'No.'

'So why are you here?'

'I wanted to meet you. I'm going to marry your daughter.'

'You must be mad. Come in. I'll tell you a few things about

my Nance.' He chuckled. 'Follow your nose along the passage to the distillery. The sunlight's in there at the moment. I want to get a good look at you.'

'I assure you I'm quite normal.'

'We all think we're that. I'll give you my professional opinion as soon as I've examined you. To your left, young man, and be careful where you tread. I only tidy up once a month.'

The small red strips of faded floral carpet were like islands in a sea of bottles. I stepped from island to island until I stood, surrounded by glinting glass, in the centre of the room.

'If you'd called tomorrow, the floor would have been clear. It's the thirty-first today.'

'You drink a lot?'

'My, you're astute. I drink a lot. I'm not an alcoholic, though, because I always have my wits about me. Chuck those empties out of the armchair and sit down.'

I removed three bottles, and the sea came closer.

'You'll join me in a tipple?'

'Yes, thank you, Mr Williams.'

'Cider's my potion.' He sang shakily, in a music-hall approximation of a West Country accent: ' "Oi've just come up from Zummerzet where the zoider apples grow." '

He manœuvred his way — a side-step here; a jump there — to a shabby kitchen barely concealed by a bead curtain. 'The Casbah,' he said, setting the beads rattling. 'Ooo la la.' He reappeared, carrying two mugs and a quart bottle. 'It's not often I entertain a guest. Will I make it to base?'

More side-steps, more jumps — 'If this was an event in the Olympics, I'd win the gold medal every time' — and he was standing in front of me.

'Keeps the old legs in trim. *Mens sana in corpore sano.* Take the green one — it commemorates Queen Victoria's jubilee. Without its cracks, it would be worth a few pence. On second thoughts, take the other one instead. Her Majesty had shaving-soap inside her yesterday, and I'm not very thorough when it comes to washing up.'

He poured the drinks. He seated himself opposite me, on a wobbly table.

'Before I salute you in apple juice, there's something I have to do. I must part with my pearlies for a while.'

He removed his false teeth, wrapped them in a grubby handkerchief, and put them in his pocket.

A grizzled baby now, he explained: 'The dentist made them too close together. Booze doesn't go through them like it should. I take them out when I'm supping. Cheers.'

'Cheers.'

'What's your name?'

'Peter Smart.'

'So she'll be Nancy Smart, will she? How is my little girl? How is my Nance?'

'She's well.'

'Did you meet her in that home she was in? Where they gave her the treatment?'

'No. I met her at a party.'

'She goes to parties these days, does she?'

'Yes.'

'And she *is* well? Not just her body?'

'Yes, Mr Williams, she is.'

'Is she still spinning her yarns?'

'She does tell the occasional fib.'

'Occasional? Fib? She *must* have changed. Do you mean to say she's stopped telling the world and his wife how she was raped when she was twelve?'

'She told me she was fourteen.'

He spluttered. 'She did, did she? Adding a few years, is she? Did she mention where it happened?'

'Kew Gardens.'

'Among the rhododendrons?'

'No. Behind a eucalyptus.'

'French sailors, were they, with pompoms on their hats?'

'No. A man with a goatee beard—'

'Oh yes. He used to crop up in all manner of places.'

'—and a Chinaman with a pigtail.'

'She has imagination, I'll say that for my Nance. She's been raped all over London, according to her. Except for the top of Nelson's Column, there's nowhere she hasn't been assaulted.

She was very partial to the Tower at one time. Every Tom, Dick and Harry must have heard how a beefeater slipped it to her in a dungeon when he should have been showing the tourists round. Nance tickled me pink with her stories.'

'You laughed at her?'

'Bloody sure I did. I took the view that healthy laughter would discourage her. It didn't, though. She got worse. Before she went into the home, she was accosting strangers in the street and asking them why they'd treated her so brutally. No, laughter didn't work with her, as it does with most. Does she hate me, Peter Smart?'

'She hasn't said so.'

'What has she said then? Did she give you my address?'

'After much persuasion.'

'I bet. No more shilly-shallying — let me have the truth, pure and simple.'

'She wants to forget that you exist.'

'She'll have to want on, won't she? I'd oblige her if I could, but there's no way I can.'

'I'm sure she doesn't mean it.'

'You can't be sure of anything with Nance — that you *can* be sure of. Hold your mug out. There's gallons more in the casbah. Has Dolly's name ever come up in your conversations?'

'No, Mr Williams.'

'Dolly's her mother.'

'Who ran away?'

'She didn't run away. Doll was no fly-by-night. She was built to make her fortune in Soho, but she was faithful to me to the last. The morning of November the third 1952, she let me sow my oats as usual — she was never the refusing kind — and after we were done, I went and made a pot of strong tea and buttered her toast for her, and set them out nicely on a tray with a napkin, and carried it into the bedroom. "Sit up, you dozy cow," I said. "Stir yourself." She was to do no more stirring, Mr Smart.'

He pulled out his handkerchief to dry his eyes. His teeth fell into his lap. He laughed.

'I sold the business — I was a grocer — and brought up my lying little Nance as best I could. My best wasn't good enough. No, not by a long bloody chalk.'

'Will you come to our wedding?'

'Not a chance.'

'I'd like you to.'

'Yes, but she wouldn't. Her wish is my command.'

In the hallway, as I was leaving, he clutched my hands and stared at me intently. 'Are you sure you weren't in that home?'

'Positive.'

'She needs someone who knows which world he's living in.'

'I'll give her your love.'

'Don't give her something she doesn't want.'

'She's pregnant, by the way.'

'By the way? Not by the beefeater or the Chinaman?'

'No. Me.'

'I believe you. Shove off now. Drop me a line when I'm a grandfather.'

'You *must* stop telling lies. Especially to me.'

'I'll try, Peter.'

'You weren't raped; your mother didn't run away, and you're not half Russian.'

'I never said I was.'

'You did.'

'When did I?'

'The night I didn't push you.'

'My mind was all to pieces. I was in one of my states. I could have said anything.'

'I forgive you.'

'Do you always speak the truth, Peter?'

'Almost always.'

'Tell me you love me. You haven't yet.'

'I love you,' I lied.

'I love you too. On my life I love you.'

★

'I've bought a small house in Clapham.'

'A charming area, I believe. Full of old socialists with beards.'

'You must visit us.'

'Only in a coffin.'

'Neville—'

'For Christ's sake, Peter, stop it. The very sight of your bride-to-be brings me out in a rash. I trust my instinct, and my instinct says "Beware!"'

'How melodramatic of it.'

'I hope you suffer for marrying her. You deserve to. You're only doing it for the sake of your soul. No, not even that. You're doing it to prove to yourself that you're a good, decent human being who really cares for the waifs and strays.'

I saw Wagner Furious speeding towards me, and ducked. It scratched Frida Leider's chest, but no further harm was done.

'Well, you're married now, You.'

'Yes, Mother.'

'I suppose I ought to give you my congratulations.'

'Thank you.'

'Not much of a turn out, was it? You two don't seem to have many friends.'

'If they aren't ill, they're on holiday.'

'In October? Trust your friends to be different from everyone else's. Who's that individual with the cigar glued to his teeth?'

'He's my agent.'

'The only agents I've heard of are spies.'

'He finds me work.'

'And he charges you for it?'

'Naturally.'

'It doesn't sound natural to me, but then nothing much does any more. I find life a puzzle, and I ache in every joint.'

'Are you sure you won't have something to drink?'

'You should know me and alcohol by now, You. I've never got on with the filthy stuff. What you could do is to ask your wife if she'd care to make me a cup of good English tea in her brand new kitchen.'

'I'll make it, Mother.'

'You? I was brought up to believe that women did the cooking.'

'Making tea isn't cooking.'

'It was classed as such in my day.'

I offered her broken Pekoe and she snorted. 'That was the old stoat's brew. Horrible scented muck. Mention of him reminds me that I shall be on the move in the near future, God willing. I'm selling The Elms.'

'Why?'

'That's the twenty-fifth letter. Because I feel lost in it. Those rooms are big enough to roam in. It's a bus ride from one end of my lounge to the other. And besides, Kensington isn't as respectable as it used to be. There was an Arab in the butcher's last Tuesday, wearing a robe.'

'Will you stay in London?'

'No, I will not. Bournemouth's my destination. I intend to be happy and healthy for a change. I'm looking forward to bracing winds from off the sea and no black faces.'

'There are some books of the doctor's I'd like, Mother, if it's all right with you.'

'Of course it is. I've no need of the rubbish. You can come and ransack his temple whenever you want to.'

Nancy swelled and became almost beautiful. Her bright eyes looked outward. She beamed down at her belly. In those long weeks before Stephen's birth she ceased to be a creature of violent contrasts. Whiteness and redness merged. Nothing disturbed her.

'I'm complete,' she said.

There was no insistence in her voice. She was stating a fact. Then her labour began.

'It's killing me, Peter. It's killing me.'

'I'll get you to hospital. The pain will soon be over.'

And so said the nurse who met us. So said the sister in charge. So said the doctor. We all gave her the same words of comfort.

'I can't bear it, Peter.'

'Yes, you can, Mrs Smart,' said the nurse. 'It's in a good cause, remember.'

The 'good cause' didn't allow her to forget. The night passed slowly. At seven in the morning, after much inducement, the baby appeared, bit by bloody bit, to the accompaniment of his mother's screams.

I saw, through glass, the new body cut loose. First slap, first cry, first wash: I put my wet hands to my wet eyes when the ritual was completed.

'Take him, Mrs Smart dear.'

'Not now.'

I looked up. I saw Nancy turn away from her son.

Nancy's depression, the doctor assured me, was perfectly normal. It was understandable that she should reject a child whose birth had been so agonizing for her. I was to be patient. I was to wait.

I was patient, and I waited. While Nancy brooded, wandering from room to room, I tended to Stephen's needs. I fed him, bathed him, changed and washed his nappies. I comforted him when he cried, and rocked him to sleep. Whenever I left the house, Stephen in his pram went with me.

On the first of every month — when dull violets and duller roses covered the floor and made walking easy — I took him to see his grandfather.

'Let me have him. The old soak's sober, Peter — don't worry yourself. Is Nance in the dumps still?'

'Yes, George.'

'And she's still not talking to my little friend here?'

'No, she's not.'

'Fetch us some juice from the casbah. You have a right, if anyone has, to drown your sorrows.'

I drank enough to nourish them then. The long, slow drowning happened later.

'Now you're better, Nancy, pay him some attention.'

'You give him all the attention he needs. And more. I wish you gave me half as much.'

'Oh, I do. I do.'

'No, you don't.'

'You can't be jealous of your own son.'

'Yes, I can—if I'm made to be. There he is, bawling for you. Go to him, Peter.'

'You go instead.'

'It's Da-da he wants.'

'Nancy, please go to him.'

'That bloody noise is getting on my nerves. Give him his cuddle, Peter, and shut him up.'

'You can't be so cruel.'

'I can be jealous and cruel and anything I want to be.'

'Think of Stephen. Stop thinking of yourself.'

'Peter, he's screaming.'

'You know what to do about it.'

'Be kind to me, Peter. Give me time. Just this once, you go.'

I went, of course. In our small, sparsely furnished, brightly painted house in Clapham I cared for my blond, healthy son. I was both mother and father to him.

Stephen began to speak, and became a person. For Nancy, he became a challenge, too—he was no longer a thing that gurgled or bawled. He had to be addressed. He demanded recognition.

He got it. I recognized its nature. I wasn't convinced when she kissed him good night and told him she loved him. Nor was he. He wiped away her kisses with the back of a tiny hand. Mine he was happy to retain.

For Stephen's sake I endured domestic bliss. I played the role of loving husband for his benefit, not Nancy's. When Mother snapped, Father made light of it; while Mummy sat in gloomy silence, Daddy chatted, or told tall stories; when Mum couldn't be bothered, Dad was solicitous: tolerance, trust, stability were the virtues I assumed. It was a performance—I hoped; I hoped fervently—of casual, unremarkable naturalness. It would be a rock of sorts for my son to build on one day.

But even the best parts pall when played constantly: with

Stephen at school, I was tempted to remove my benevolent mask and substitute another more expressive of my true feelings. Yet as soon as I donned the mask marked Rage I let it slip, for fear of the consequences. Nancy, whom I'd made complete for a time, had been hurt enough. She'd been in a mental institution; she'd had electric treatment. Weren't there scars on her wrists? I re-adjusted Benevolence.

Whisky enabled me to sustain the act. I drank it, often in the Russian style, in a number of hiding places – the bathroom, the cellar, the garden shed. It gave a certain glow to the performance, and it smoothed the works.

I sucked a lot of peppermints, to kill the smell.

'Peter, you're not going.'

'Nancy, I am.'

'You're not to go. You can't.'

'Tell me why.'

'I'm helpless by myself. I can't cope. I can't face things.'

'You'll cope, love. You will.'

'You're a terrible actor, anyway. It's a waste of your time.'

'Nancy – I want to return to the stage. It's only for a few weeks. I'm sick of just doing bits and pieces, coughs and spits, for television. Please understand that I need to be in the theatre again.'

'But why leave London?'

'Because I've been offered a tour.'

'You're running away from me.'

'I've told you – it's only for a few weeks.'

'And what about *him*?'

'Who is "him"?'

'The one who pisses his bed every night.'

'The one I'm constantly assuring he's done nothing to be ashamed of? The one whose sheets I wash?'

'The one of the two of us you love more.'

'Oh, Nancy, you're talking nonsense. I'm tired of listening to it. So what about Stephen?'

'I'm not looking after him.'

'You never have done. Now's your chance to do so. It will be good for you, as well as a surprise for him.'

'You can take him with you. He'll applaud you, if no one else does.'

'You know I can't take him. You know that, Nancy.'

'You'll turn down the job, then? You'll stay?'

I told her—calmly, quietly—that I was determined to go.

'In that case, I might not be here when you come back.'

'What does that mean, Nancy?'

'It means I might not be here when you come back.'

'Where will you be?'

She stared at me. She smiled. Then she removed her caftan and stood naked. She put my hands on to her buttocks and wrapped her arms round me. 'I still love you, Peter. Come on.'

Releasing myself, I said, 'You show your love in strange ways. I think I'd prefer it if you were occasionally considerate instead. Why don't you cook dinner tonight? Practice makes perfect, you know. Or is it the lady of leisure's intention to hire a chef during her husband's absence?'

'I'm as bad at cooking as you are at acting.'

'I try to improve—that's the difference between us. Put my pinny on, and learn. You can call me when you've burnt the steak. I shall be in the cellar.'

Nancy remained at home with Stephen while I added lustre in provincial towns and cities. The play, described by the management as a frothy comedy, was called *The Captivating Shrimp*. I was dapper Roddy Robson-Phillips—blazer and white flannels by St Laurent—whose pursuit of pert Priscilla, the not quite youthful daughter of impecunious, but entirely lovable Lord Comstock and his dotty wife, the Lady Ambrosine, is hampered by the fact that her hand in matrimony has been pledged to the brash Texan oil millionaire, Hiram J. Hamburger III, whose generous donation to the Save Castle Comstock Fund has guaranteed that the stately pile won't be seized by 'those damned Bolshevists in Westminster'. 'Roddy, I'll *have* to marry the noisy brute – after all, he's saved dear old dads from bankruptcy. It's a terrible dilemma, it really is. He looks a perfect fright on a horse.' Plunged into something like despair by this announcement, Roddy asks the butler, Meredith, to mix him a 'knockout snifter'. Meredith obliges, and after three more of same, Roddy falls to the floor, taking an antique screen with him. Meredith, adopting a disdainful expression, exits. Enter, chirpily, the new maidservant, diminutive Brenda Bloggs, the shrimp of the title, who awakens Roddy with a less than decorous kiss: 'Beg pardon, Your Honour, but in my humble you're a smasher.' Romance blooms, though Roddy tries to resist it at first. 'It's no go, Roddy old lad,' he tells himself, 'a Robson-Phillips getting spliced to a Bloggs – it wouldn't look right, next to the Court Circular.' Later in the play, Meredith – an avid student of the *Almanach da Gotha, Debrett*, and *Burke's Peerage* – reveals to the assembled cast (excepting the 'shrimp', who is 'doing' elsewhere) his suspicions about 'that young Miss Bloggs, who is now so very much in our midst'. The word 'suspicions' puts Lady Ambrosine into a tizzy: 'You don't mean, do you, Meredith – no, no, no, no, you can't – that this Biggs or Baggs girl is a common thief?' 'Hardly *common*,' replies the butler, with feeling. 'And scarcely a thief. It was her facial resemblance to the Zoffany portrait of Emily, Lady Pike, in the Blue Room that gave me the clue. Your maidservant, Madam, is the daughter of Lord Arthur Pike, who disappeared in mysterious circumstances some twenty years ago following an assault on his person in a gaming establishment. Suffering from amnesia, he gave himself the soubriquet Bloggs and settled in a London suburb with a female person of distinctly low origins. The Honourable Brenda Pike was the outcome of their union ... ' With the course of true love now running smooth, Roddy and Brenda make their wedding plans, and Priscilla staunchly agrees to marry Hiram: 'He's not so bad, I suppose. How can I stop him wearing those frightful tartan suits?' The play ends with Priscilla fighting back tears and saying to Roddy 'Ridiculous, isn't it, Rods? You're joining the Pike family – they're freshwater, I think – and I'm becoming a Hamburger.' To which Roddy replies 'But a Hamburger, Priscilla, made with the best roast beef of old England. And although I'm marrying a Pike she'll always be a shrimp to me.'

The tour took me to Bournemouth.

'Did you enjoy it, Mother?'

'I smiled here and there, on and off. I thought everyone was real, except you.'

'What was the matter with me?'

'You'd soon know if you could watch yourself.'

'And what does that mean?'

'You weren't five minutes out of your cot before you started to be a pest with questions. I didn't think you were natural. You reminded me too much of your father.'

I was startled, and flattered, and speechless.

'He was awkward in clothes as well,' she explained. 'I never saw him at ease in them. A suit and Gerald Smart were seldom friends for long. Where are you staying?'

'In a hotel.'

'With gold taps in the bathrooms, I don't doubt. If you care to walk along the front one afternoon, you might stop and honour me with a visit during your stay.'

'Yes, of course I shall.'

'I suppose I must thank you for the ticket. You're not eating enough. Doesn't that Nancy feed you?'

'I'll tell you when I honour you with a visit, Mother.'

'Miserable news, eh? Any afternoon will do. You remember where I live?'

'Yes, of course I do.'

'You were the spitting image of him out there tonight. In a quandary you were, and that's the truth. Yes, you're the son of your father. There's next to nothing of me in you. I'll be off now.'

'I'll show you to the stage door.'

'All these lights, all those mirrors — it's unnatural. What a life for a grown man! Good night then, Roddy.'

'Peter, Mother.'

'It says "Hugh" outside. I'll shake the dust off the welcome mat for when you come. I'd take in some fresh air in the meantime, if I were you, You.'

Mother's flat overlooked the sea. 'I like to watch it when it's in a turmoil,' she said. 'I feel that bit warmer and cosier in here.'

There was warmth, certainly – an electric fire, with brightly flickering imitation logs, made sure of that. There was cosiness, too: the chintz-covered armchair I sank into was more comfortable than anything I had ever sat on in Ranley Road or The Elms. Cheerful one-eyed pirates, lascivious straw-sucking ostlers, and rosy-cheeked, stomach-patting squires leered, winked and grinned at me from all directions.

'I've taken to collecting jugs, in case you hadn't noticed, You.'

'Yes, Mother, I had.'

'They're proper characters, aren't they? Whenever I buy a new one, I give him a name. The individual by my sewing-box at your elbow I christened Dirty Dick. I wouldn't trust him on a dark night, I can tell you. Dirty Dick – meet my son.'

I was introduced, in turn, to Boastful Bertrand, Happy Horace, Mischievous Michael, Cut-throat Cuthbert, Saucy Sam, Jaunty Jack, and a dozen others.

'They keep me company, in their way.'

'You had a budgerigar the last time I came.'

'Oh, he, she, or it's still around. It's the same nuisance it always was – silent as the tomb when you're in the mood for a chat; screaming its head off when you want peace and quiet. You never know where you are with the thing.'

I was left with her amiable rogues while she prepared tea. I tried to ignore them. I picked up a book: beneath the unchanging desert sky, Chloe finally succumbed to the Bedouin's demands. I willed myself not to weep.

Mother called from the kitchen. 'Can you stir yourself to push the trolley in? I'm an old lady now, and I'm shaky on my pins, I hate to say.'

I went to her assistance.

'Polly wants a cracker,' said the budgerigar.

'Trust you to speak when you're not spoken to. Shut up, Thing.'

'Polly wants a cracker!'

'It was me saying "trolley" set it off. They're the only words it knows: Polly's been wanting her perishing cracker from the day I bought it. Let's get back among the boys.'

Among the boys again, we ate and drank. I consumed a heap of cucumber sandwiches, slab after slab of fruit cake.

'I can't imagine why I'm so hungry.'

'I can. Misery's the reason.'

'Is it?' I asked, wanting to hear more.

'It is. It always was, with you. You used to eat with a vengeance when you had the glooms. Oh, you'd shovel food in then. Have you been up to your daft tricks lately?'

'Daft tricks, Mother?'

'With string tied to the banister? Waiting for slates to fall and flatten you? Those kind of tricks.'

'No. I haven't been up to those.'

'I should hope not. I remember the first one you played on me. You were a toddler. You let go of my hand and ran into the middle of the road. Then you lay on the ground, with cars and buses and such dodging past you – only inches away from you, some of them were. You lay there out of spite. I tanned your hide off when I got you home. I said to your free and easy father that you had a devil inside you, but he laughed it off, like he did everything.'

'Yes, Mother, I am miserable.'

'You'll get no help from this quarter, You. God helps those who help themselves – that's what I was brought up to believe. No one – not one single living soul – has ever helped Ellen Dixon, or Smart as she became, for her sins. She learned not to ask for it, so she wasn't disappointed when she didn't receive it.'

'I only came to see you – not to ask for help.'

'Well, I'm not offering it, so let that be understood. I'm too busy propping myself up to spare a peg for you.'

We were silent. I stared into my tea cup. Then, almost glee-fully, Mother asked: 'Is she giving you hell?'

Surprised by the question, and by her tone of voice, I simply looked at her. Before I could answer no, she continued: 'I knew she would. She was determined to.'

'I thought you approved of her.'

'I didn't say I didn't, if I recall. I was speaking a truth. I knew, as soon as I clapped eyes on her, that she'd give you hell. You're on the run from her, aren't you, You? That's why you're here.'

'I ring her every day, to find out how she is. And Stephen.'

'If he survives the pair of you, he'll be able to stand on his own two feet and no mistake.'

'He will.'

'You don't have to shout. Is he drawing diagrams yet?'

'He draws.'

'I have to laugh when I think of you locking yourself into the old stoat's temple to write what you called your masterpiece. There were more squiggles than words.'

'You read it?'

'What there was of it to read. I took an interest in you once, you'll be amused to know. You haven't improved with age.'

'Thank you, Mother,' I said, allowing habit to rule over judgment.

'You were born sarcastic, you were, You. You ought to listen to yourself say "Mother" — you've never made it sound natural, at least not to my ears. Still, it's too late now to expect you to change. I shouldn't believe it if you did. Yes, it's too late in the day for you to start behaving like a son to me. What's more, I honestly don't think I want you to.'

'In that case, Mother,' I said, 'I shan't.'

'Trying to cure you of pride was a full time job for me. Oh, you used to rile me with your stuck-up airs. I had to laugh the day I overheard you talking to Sir Peter. Sir Peter was you, wasn't he? Sir Peter! You're not Sir Anybody now, are you? Being Roddy for the benefit of the snobs who live in these parts isn't anything special, is it?'

'No. Nothing special.'

'It isn't much for a man in his thirties to be proud of, is it?'

'No. It isn't much.'

'Not when you consider. You haven't done as well out of life as you expected to, have you?'

'I suppose I haven't.'

'You suppose! Listen to him, boys — just listen. You're not to mock him, Horace—and I'd be obliged if you kept a civil tongue in your head, Sam. Manners, boys, manners.'

Conceding defeat with a shrug, I sat on. Mother smirked; Mother gloated; Mother crowed. The malicious, I decided, have a dark happiness. It sustains and fortifies them; it ensures their survival.

There were no further triumphs for Mother that afternoon. After her caution to Horace and Sam, she became predictable again: I was told who invented steam, and which letter was twenty-fifth in the alphabet. Horses were mentioned, and cursed. So were Dr Cottie, the government, the citizens of Bournemouth, and the budgerigar—who, chirping twice, was twice told to shut up.

We exchanged brisk goodbyes. Then Mother opened *Oasis o. Ecstasy*, sniffed it, and began to read.

'I warned you not to go away.'
'Yes, you did, Nancy. You certainly did.'
'It won't take you long to clear up the mess.'
'About a week, by the look of it.'
'Aren't you lucky? You needn't pay me any attention until next Sunday.'
'Nancy, where's my tobacco jar?'
'It broke.'
'How?'
'It fell out of my hands.'
'And where's the fruit bowl?'
'That broke too.'
'It fell out of your hands?'
'No. I threw it at the wall. Can't you see the mark it made?'
'Yes, Nancy, I can. Did you break anything else?'
'Lots of things. Half the dinner service, for instance. The bathroom mirror. Your Georgian punch glasses.'
'Why, Nancy?'
'To test you. To see which you care for most—possessions or me. By the way, the postman's a very good lover.'
'Like the Chinaman? Like the French sailors?'

'No, not like them. He's real flesh and blood. Especially flesh. His cock is twice the size of yours.'

'And where was this treasure revealed to you – the Tower of London, perhaps?'

'No. Upstairs. I've grown quite accustomed to receiving my morning male in the bedroom.'

'You never forwarded my letters, Nancy, Where are they?'

'I tore them all up. I read them first, and then I tore them up. I warned you not to go away. You should have told me you were queer.'

'What do you mean?'

'You should have told me. You let me fall in love with you; you put me through all that pain, and you didn't tell me – not once. Here's his letter. I tore it up, but thinking you'd want to read it, I stuck it together again. Wasn't that kind of me?'

The letter was from the long forgotten Wolfram: how well he remembered the hearty breakfast I had so generously prepared for him at four in the afternoon; how well he remembered taking my ferocious love-bites back to Darmstadt, and concealing them from his so inquisitive mother; how well he remembered every little thing there was to remember about that enchanted occasion in the so beautiful capital of England, to which he would be returning shortly for a conference on Abyssinian art …

'Isn't he affectionate?'

'Yes, Nancy.'

'Will you be seeing him?'

'Definitely.'

'You bastard.'

'I'm too weary, Nancy, to reason with you. I'll go and bath our son.'

'You do that. Can you tell him he won't be visiting his grandfather any more?'

'Why?'

'Because he won't.'

'Has something happened to George?'

'Only death.'

'Nancy, are you lying?'

'You cured me of lying. I didn't go to his funeral. I had my period that day.'

'You could have told me.'

'You could have told me too. I saved the news for your home-coming.'

'Daddy,' Stephen said when I kissed him good night, 'your mouth smells. Your hands are all wobbly. I'd like a different Mummy. You're crying.'

It was my turn, now, to have a kiss removed.

At ten the following morning the doorbell rang. The postman was on the step.

'Oh. Er. Oh,' he said.

'Yes?'

'I sort of thought I'd let you know there isn't any post for you today.'

'How very courteous.'

'If — er — you have a small parcel tomorrow, or a letter, I'll be sure to deliver it.'

'Isn't that your job?'

'So to speak. Yes.'

'That *is* your knee, isn't it, where your knee should be?'

'I hope so. I didn't have a wooden leg when I got dressed.'

'A wooden leg would present problems, would it?'

'Oh, yes. I mean, with the miles I walk and the weight I carry.'

'I do sympathize. Aren't most artificial limbs made of metal these days?'

'I think they are. They're lighter, of course. Not so cumbersome.'

'I simply must compliment you on your right knee-cap.'

'Thanks. The left one suits me fine as well.'

'I assume you've never suffered from *genu valgum*?'

'No. Not at all. Not to my knowledge. Not in the least. No.'

'Do you wear shorts in the summer?'

'On the beach, yes. In Spain.'

'Not on your rounds?'

'Oh, no. It wouldn't be proper.'

'What a pity. Am I to be deprived, then, of the sight of it?'

'My knee?'

'What else?'

'I'll show it to you if you like.'

'Come inside. We don't want the neighbours commenting.'

In the hall, the smiling postman lowered his trousers. I inspected the shapely knee. And yes, I had cured Nancy of lying. Just.

'This is a funny house. This really is a funny house.'

I'd have voiced my agreement, but my foul-smelling mouth was full.

In a Bloomsbury hotel, Herr Professor Bonn and I did our best to recapture the enchantment of yesteryear. We did not succeed, despite the fierceness of our love-making. Wolfram was bald and fat and had difficulty breathing; I was skinnier than ever, grey faced, grey haired, and drunk. We set ourselves to abandonment with a purpose.

'Peter, we must stop a moment. I must up for air come. I am gulping like some big fish. There is more of me for you to bite into, yes?'

'Yes, Wolfram.'

'I am, I hope, cuddly.'

With eyes closed, I saw the apple tree, the hanged prisoner. I saw a boy transfixed.

'Such strength. Such stamina. I enjoy.'

I returned to Clapham very drunk.

'There's a Sergeant Kemp in the kitchen. He has some news for you.'

Sergeant Kemp's news made me sober in an instant.

Cut-throat Cuthbert and his shipmates welcomed me back. Dick and Sam had had the best view of my mother's rotting week-old corpse. They were smiling still.

'Heave-ho, my hearties.'

I sat in the chair she'd died in and opened the box containing her private papers. On the top were ancient rent books and ration books, identity cards, receipts, telegrams—a hoarder's junk. I searched the stuff, without success, for secrets.

Beneath some bags of lavender, there were photographs. I saw my father, looking uncharacteristically spirited, in uniform, in Flanders: a man of fortitude; a man of action. I saw him— stooped, grim-featured—in the grounds of a hospital, a beaming nurse at his side: a man with more than outward injuries: a man dismayed by the pictures in his head. I saw him on his wedding day: a man out of temper with his clothes, but smiling valiantly, in accord with the occasion. I saw him, and wondered when he'd acquired his talent for vanishing.

Mother and the camera had maintained a mutually distrustful relationship. She'd stared at the lens and defied it to capture her malign individuality. In every snapshot, her face was a blur. Nothing of her sharpness, her forcefulness, had registered. Granite had been softened into blancmange.

I saw myself as Lady Macbeth, examining the little hand which all the perfumes of Arabia could not sweeten. Had my Gentle-woman and my Doctor discovered, as I was discovering, that Hell is murky? Blazered and flannelled Roddy had cavorted there, in the half-light.

Then I read a postcard:

My dearest Nellie. Your visit did me a power of good. You are always kind to me. I would like to see Gerald and the Boy but not in here. I have eaten the fruit you gave me. You made me laugh about the tramp. You are always patient with your loving Mother.

Then, from the bottom of the box, I brought out a truss. A note was attached to it, in Mother's handwriting: 'Gerald's. 1946. The fool.'

I wanted to smash Horace and Bertrand and Jack—her boon companions—but didn't. Their laughter seemed appropriate.

I went down to the sea. The budgerigar had earned a sailor's burial.

In Clapham, months later, a drunken coward, I left my wife a note. I told her of my desperation, in words similar to these:

I have to go. I can no longer endure your love — if love it is. I feel trapped and suffocated. I need to breathe.

I am going for your sake too. I am taking a risk, I know. Haven't you said a thousand times that you'll kill yourself if I leave you? Well, I must take that risk. You must find a need to live that doesn't involve me. And you must be a mother to Stephen before it's too late.

When I first met you (or rescued you), you had a job as a secretary. Why don't you go out and get another? Meet people. Make some friends. Forget yourself.

I can't support you any more, and I don't mean financially. For years, Nancy, I've been cruel to you with misplaced kindness. I was drawn to you only by pity, and I'm now drained of it. The supply has run out.

Keep the house clean. Weed the garden. Please dispose of the bottles in the shed.

There is nearly a thousand pounds in the bank. I've drawn out enough for myself.

Face the challenge.

I shall contact you when I feel capable. See that Stephen eats plenty of fresh vegetables. Help him with his spelling.

Don't attempt to follow me. I have no definite destination.

PETER

I refrained from saying goodbye to Stephen. He, too, would be better without my boozy presence. The rock of sorts was on the point of crumbling.

The clerk in the booking-office at King's Cross asked me a third time to say where I was going.

'North,' I said.

'The north is large. It has lots of towns and cities.'

'Send me among the heathens,' I said.

'Heathen, surely. What about Darlington? I've heard it's picturesque.'

'Then Darlington it is. Darlington it must be.'

On the train, my escape certain, I called myself a shit. 'You shit,' I muttered. 'You complete and utter shit.' But weren't there, I reasoned, degrees of shittiness? I wasn't in the Goering class, after all. Hardly 'complete and utter'. There was a shit in every house in every street, and some of them had spectacular credentials. I was a pretty average example of the breed. The Caligula Cross for Craps was still out of my reach.

I sat beneath a willow and looked up at the Victorian Gothic mansion in which my other grandmother had lived for thirty years. I watched as troops of patients took their morning exercise in the grounds. I imagined Mother offering them her annual, awkward comfort, and Mrs Dixon breaking ranks to curtsey her gratitude.

— You were born sarcastic.

All of a sudden, all the marching patients looked like Nancy. I fled.

BORDERS WELCOME, I read, and entered. In the dingy, kipper-scented vestibule of the San Remo Guest House, I spoke to Mr Sandison, its owner. 'The terms are most reasonable,' he observed as I halted the progress of his floor-bound body. 'The best in Edinburgh.' He swayed before me. 'The very best.' We shook hands on the agreement. 'Angus will show you to your room.'

Although his master was now caressing the carpet, surly Angus did. I tipped him generously, to his obvious displeasure. He counted the coins into a purse, told me that only southern Jessies put sugar in porridge, and left me to savour the delights of my new home.

What sights greeted me, and how my heart lifted! This was paradise: eau-de-nil lino; yellow walls; a rusty iron bedstead; a cracked enamel bowl, with a thick scum mark all the way round it; oh, and yes—the inevitable walnut wardrobe, with the inevitable piece of brown paper stuffed between the door and the jamb; a dressing-table, complete with mirror—its glass obscured by paint spots; a light bulb dangling from the centre of the ceiling, with a torn pink shade ... I blessed the decorator. That man, or woman, had known real desolation of spirit.

Those objects had been stored for someone's ruin, and someone had arrived.

Elated, I peered under the bed. Joy of joys—a po! And unemptied, too—cigarette stubs had turned the piss a deep orange colour. Truly, Mr Sandison's 'tairms' were extremely reasonable. Pulling back the frayed curtain, I took in the view: blackened brick; nothing else. Excessively reasonable.

Each afternoon, I stepped over the fly-blown proprietor of the San Remo and walked for a while in the city. I seldom went far from the Grassmarket, where the guest house was situated. One day, drunk as usual, I found myself in front of a Temperance hall. Why was it familiar? I remembered, eventually. In that gaunt building, long ago, I had added lustre in a verse play called *Evening Dress Essential*, which had attracted two kilts, several dirndl skirts, and acres of corduroy during the course of the Festival. Forgotten now, it had been compared to Shakespeare and the Jacobeans at its first production. I had played Cedric, whose scene with the haunted Lydia in Act Two (prior to her death on off-stage Popocatepetl) was considered the high point of the drama:

CEDRIC. *Shadows outpace us. These, Lydia, are dark times*
    We live in.
LYDIA. *Dark, Cedric,*
    Dark. The world turns on its axis
    Darkly.
CEDRIC. *Even as we speak*
    The worm is at his business in the bud.
LYDIA. *Busy devourer! Taking tea this morning—*
    You know my passion for Darjeeling, dear—
    I thought I caught the sound of rattling bones.
CEDRIC (impulsively). *I heard them too! Battling through the crowd*
    At Fortnum's, for my special foie gras,
    I caught their rattle.
LYDIA (bitterly). *A battle? For a rattle?*
    Grim jest! (Starts.) *Oh, do I hear them still?*
CEDRIC/LYDIA. *Darkly,*
    We listen.

CEDRIC (after a pause, gloomily). *Lydia, Lydia,*
I have heard their sound, their rattle,
In the dread desert wastes.
In the dread desert wastes
(Over a cocktail after coitus)
Those bones echoed round me.

LYDIA (mysteriously). *Cedric, Cedric,*
At this violet hour,
I can hear
Their echo.

CEDRIC. *In Africa last spring—*
While on a mission for the Foreign Office—
I forgot the squeaking of pens, the taping of Reds,
And paid a visit to a lazaretto.
The lepers' sores
Blaze for me yet, in Hampstead.
Yes, Lydia, they burn.

LYDIA. *Cedric, Cedric,*
I can feel
That heat.

CEDRIC (casually, lighting a cigarette). *Please, Lydia,*
Do not upset yourself. Look on the bright
Side. Yesterday, wasn't it, your shares
Rose on the Stock Exchange?
I shall ring for drinks.
A gin and tonic, is it?

LYDIA. *Thank you,*
Cedric (prophetically). *Tomorrow I shall book*
A cabin—first class, naturally—on a slow boat
Destined for the Americas. I shall be reborn
In the Mexican Gulf. There, only there,
Shall I find the whole.

CEDRIC. *But for tonight*
Let us drink and be merry. Sir Percy's Rolls
Is in the drive already. Here's Cynthia too.
And old Lord Fortescue!
Lydia, Lydia, I forgot to say
You look superb in lilac ...

Returning to the room I was determined to die in, clutching my newly acquired copy of *Lo! The Trestles!*, I passed the Askmac Tourist Agency. I invited my addled brain to tell me why 'Askmac' was familiar, too. It told me nothing. I retraced my steps and read the poster in the shop window: *Proprietors— David Askew and Norman Machin. Your Satisfaction Our Concern.* So the publishers of Sister Evangeline and F. Leonard Cottie were doing well for themselves at last ...

Then a stone shattered the glass. 'Ye bloody swindlers!' shouted a wild Scots voice. 'It wasn't me,' I whispered as two strong policemen led me away. I put up no further resistance. I paid my fine with a good grace, and heard the magistrate say that I had his sympathy— 'Those men are fiends. They're devils incarnate'—but damage to property, even a property that had never been purchased, could not be condoned, nor could that foul disease, drunkenness. I promised him faithfully that I would look to the kirk for guidance and be an upright citizen once more.

I bought a stock of whisky and went back to the San Remo. Mr Sandison was almost an upright citizen as he handed me my key. Safe inside my haven, I locked the door. The living were outside; I was joining the dead.

They made diverting company. Under the pink shade, my father proved to be a most substantial ghost. To hear him address the United Nations was to experience a rare filial pride. The people of San Remo, he declared with passionate conviction, could not be overlooked—they had rights; they had claims on the world's attention; if you pricked them, they bled. When the delegates rose to applaud him, so did I. 'He has the gift of tongues,' said Dr Cottie. 'He is the finest orator since Sir Royston Hammond.'

'Of fond memory.'

'Aha! You knew him?'

'I knew him, F. Leonard. I heard him lecture on disorders of the cranium.'

'His death, like my own, was cerebrovascular.'

'Mine was sudden,' said Mother. 'Mine was quick. I didn't

linger, causing trouble for others. I wish your father would stop talking, Peter.'

'Peter?'

'Have you forgotten your own name, Peter dear?'

'Upstairs with you, Nellie, my angel. I wish to emulate the *putorius ermineus*. Off with your bodice this minute.'

'You're a positive glutton, Lenny, I do declare. I can't satisfy your requirements with my guts in this turmoil.'

Against a background of scratched walnut, Mother farted freely now. There were no disguising coughs.

'Your stool, Peter, is it, is regular?'

'No, doctor. Not only am I a shit, I'm also a capricious crapper. I am very irregular. I always have been.'

'Adders of lustre should be disciplined in their habits.'

'Mother, did you poison Father?'

'Your name's Reynaldo, not Hamlet. It's time you knew your place in the scheme of things, my lad. Oh, there's that Polonius ringing for service again. Will you go, or shall I?'

My muted trumpet was no match for Mother's bassoon.

I awoke, and saw the dead in a harsher light. I saw Walter Latham, in a similar room, his days of glory over, choking on his vomit. I saw George Williams, no longer afloat on that glinting sea, and remembered how, whenever we passed an undertaker's on our walks with Stephen, he'd raise a fist and shout 'You haven't got me yet!'

They'd had him. They'd done with him.

I saw my mother among her 'boys'. Had she called for help? Had she asked, in vain, for 'Peter' or for 'You'?

I saw my green-faced father, and I saw Aunt Hilda. Edward and Alice answered them with silence.

I listened to that silence.

In the San Remo Guest House I stood up and wept.

I would leave this dump in a state fit to be seen.

I stank. However much I washed my body in Mr Sandison's hot water—and there was never that much of it—the smell wouldn't go away. I rubbed cologne into my skin, and still it was there.

I knew how to rid myself of the stink of self-absorption. I was determined to apply the cure.

My senses had been drowned enough. I made a chart: Tuesday, 4 p.m., No drink taken. 5 p.m. No drink taken. 6 p.m., 7 p.m., 8 p.m., and so on, round the clock.

From Valencia to San Remo: A spiritual tour.

Years back, Dr Cottie had said, when I'd mentioned Mother's mother, 'Disturb the balance, and chaos ensues. I have—have I not?—borne witness to that chaos.'

So had I.

I stepped over Mr Sandison for the last time.

On my way to the station, a refined lady advised me to return to Israel, where I belonged. There were too many of my kind in Scotland.

I thanked her, graciously, for her concern.

Afterword by 'Neville Drake'

'Peter Smart' gave me the manuscript of his uncompleted autobiography (along with misplaced apologies for its 'harshly in-
accurate' portrait of 'Neville Drake') a few days before his death
from cancer earlier this year. I, in turn, gave him my solemn
promise to destroy it. I should like to explain why I broke that
promise.

In the first place, I was greatly entertained by his 'trivial account of a trivial life'—not least for its horribly accurate portrait
of my erstwhile self. (The 'Wolfram' episode was particularly
diverting.) He is just as successful at capturing the uniquely
repellent character of his mother, even if his depiction occasionally errs on the side of understatement: 'Peter', being of a
charitable nature, makes her at times almost pitiable. With F.
Leonard Cottie (whom he honours with his real name—everyone
else is pseudonymous) he is at his most persuasive. 'Peter'
genuinely loved that snobbish old bore ('he was my real father',
he once exclaimed, after too much champagne) and his affection
shines through whenever 'Him upstairs' appears. (My last
present to 'Peter' was a copy of *With Stethoscope and Scalpel*
dedicated to T. S. Eliot: '*Read this, Mr Eliot, and Take Heart!
All is not Gloom. In the hope that your Muse will one day don a
brighter shift—From a Humble Medic.*')

Peter Smart's Confessions has its flaws, though. It fails to give a
convincing picture of the 'Peter' I knew and admired. Perhaps
that's due to the fact that he was plainly not at home with the
autobiographical form (only saints, monsters, and diarists writing
in code have ever succeeded with it, in my view): he hated self-
display, which is why he was such a keen observer of it in others.

187

For my taste, he mocks his considerable gift for acting to a quite annoying extent: his Bert in *The Construction* (a dramatic entertainment—it will be remembered by those who endured it—in which a council house is built, brick by brick, on stage) was a performance of great distinction, founded as it was on such unpromising material; so was his Simon in *Hold This A Moment, Darling*, whom he miraculously contrived to make believable; so, too, was his Claudio in *Measure for Measure*, the largest Shakespeare part he played; there were dozens more ... (By the way, 'Peter' worked with finer directors than that much proclaimed genius 'Hal Musgrave'. Yes, he really *did* suggest congenital syphilis as a possible explanation of Hamlet's moodiness.) I have no doubt that Peter, like his shadowy father, had a talent for vanishing—in his case, into the skins of other people. In his *Confessions* (he is not much at ease in the confessional, to his credit) he vanishes into his mother, into the doctor, into the 'Neville Drake' that was ('Drake' is very apt: I quacked, rather than talked, in my acting days) and even—to a limited extent—into 'Nancy'. His failure to convey the real 'Peter Smart' is an honourable one, but a failure nevertheless. Had he lived, he might have become a novelist. (Why, I wonder, did he choose such odd bedfellows as Thomas Mann and Jean Cocteau to praise his unwritten juvenilia? I suppose it is possible—just—to admire both of them.)

I am no writer, as my prone-to-parentheses prose clearly demonstrates. The reader who has struggled this far has probably only done so to discover what happened to the cast (the *mot juste*, I feel) of *Peter Smart's Confessions*. I hope the following list will supply her (my wife, 'Audrey', insisted on the feminine precedence) with the information he requires:

1. 'Nancy' and 'Stephen'

The *Confessions* ends with 'Peter' returning to London after a breakdown. Naturally, he went back to Clapham. (His masochistic tendencies always distressed me.) There—to his astonishment, and even, perhaps, to his relief—he found 'Nancy' in a comparatively happy state of mind. The house was moderately clean, but the garden needed weeding.

Slowly, with much effort, husband and wife became friends. 'Nancy' took a job in publishing, and eventually became an editor. (God, I should hate to be one of her authors.) Finally, when Stephen was twelve, they sold the house and separated, the boy choosing to live with his mother. The new 'Nancy' divides her affections between a Pekingese (already mentioned) and a poet, with whom she was touring Australia (he is a performer as well) at the time of her husband's death. (Her gift seems to be for avoiding funerals.)

It was 'Stephen' who precipitated his father's last, and most ridiculous, attempt at suicide. 'Peter' constantly worried about his son (excessively so – but then, I care what happens to my twin daughters): about his indifference to learning; his precocious promiscuity (Father and Son once met by accident in a V.D. clinic, to Son's considerable amusement); his lack of respect for his elders ('You're all bananas, Dad. You're all fucked up') – but these were minor worries compared to 'Stephen's' conversion. 'The day my son saw the light was the blackest of my life.' 'Peter' swallowed the overdose of canine tranquillizers after seeing his son – head shaved; face decorated with streaks of white paint; dressed in a saffron robe and sandals – selling *Back to the Godhead* in Oxford Street.

2. 'Mrs Smart'

Yes, there is something more to be said of her. In her last will and testament, she bequeathed the remainder of her inheritance from Dr Cottie to a Mr Semple, the managing director of Purrypuss Products Ltd, the cat-food manufacturers. There was a proviso, of course: 'On condition that only the insides of old horses are put into the tins.' Mr Semple refused to accept the money.

3. 'Sir Hal Musgrave'

He now has his own troupe which tours the globe with *Basic Situations*. Each night, the actors improvise certain deep-rooted human urges. Sometimes, it's sexual intercourse, in all its variety; sometimes war; sometimes boredom. (Is that an urge?) 'Words,' says 'Hal', who was rarely on speaking terms with them, 'are obsolete. Mankind must return to body-thinking.'

4. 'Neville Drake'

Thanks to the steadying influence of 'Audrey', the once extravagant 'Neville' has now – he likes to imagine – changed for the better. He teaches German in a London college, and is slowly settling his debts. He drinks champagne once a year, at Christmas: he is more used to instant coffee and orange juice. Whenever 'Audrey' and the twins are out, he listens to Wagner on his record-player.

5. 'Peter Smart'

'Peter' fell ill while writing his *Confessions*. After complaining to his doctor of tiredness, he underwent a complete physical examination. A small lump was removed from his left armpit. A biopsy revealed it to be a malignant tumour.

He returned to the hospital in which he had had a glimpse of paradise. On arrival, he asked to speak to Dr Thornton, who had treated him so contemptuously in the intensive care unit. The nurse told him that the young doctor, in a state of total despair, had thrown himself in front of a train some weeks before.

In the last months of his life – his *Confessions* abandoned – Peter read and read. He learned the names of plants and birds: 'If I manage to live, I want to know who and what I'm living with.' His enthusiasm and energy were awe-inspiring. Then, at the very end, when he was too weak to hold a book, I read to him. One letter of Cowper's he particularly loved: the poet, seeing yellow leaves falling from willows, rejects the idea of a short earthly continuance; rejects, too, the notions of heaven and hell, and simply wishes to live for ever and ever.

When he was in the mood for laughter, I read from the works of Sister Evangeline:

> *Remember, Martial,*
> *Satire is partial –*
> *O, give thy complete heart!*

and from the book that stopped a thousand doors.

(But what of those years not covered in the autobiography? Oh, dear. Well, 'Peter' foolishly abandoned acting and became a singularly inept social worker. He fell in love with a tattooed young thief named Freddy, whose charm I found hugely resistible. Oh, dear.)

'Peter' received many visitors at his bedside, including that exhausting Cockney caution, Miss Hedley, and my much-abused friend 'Serge Evanowski', whose ballet *Requiem* (inspired by the death of the dancer Barry Capes) was the one work of his that 'Peter' admired. 'Audrey' and I drank champagne with 'Peter' in the closing minutes of his life. That very day, those resilient crooks, Askew and Machin – still active in their seventies – were sentenced to several years imprisonment for smuggling illegal immigrants into the country.

6. F. Leonard Cottie

In recent months, the long dead doctor has achieved that fame he hungered after in life. His memoirs have served as the basis of a television series entitled *Surgeon to the Great*, which has had a striking success both here and in America. A sample of dialogue should indicate something of its quality:

Do you think His Excellency/Her Royal Highness/My Lord Bishop/ the Right Honourable Gentleman will pull through?
With Cottie at the helm, he/she is in with a fighting chance.

Dame Ada Keen, to whom F. Leonard Cottie bequeathed his royalties, has become a very rich old lady. She cannot appreciate her wealth since – at the age of ninety-seven – she is all but gaga in a Home.

KITTY AND VIRGIL
Paul Bailey

Kitty Crozier wakes up in a hospital ward to find a stranger looking at her. Thus begins the most important, most demanding, most exhilarating relationship of her life. The stranger's name is Florescu, a poet who has escaped from Ceausescu's Romania.

'To write a novel which lays bare tragedy alongside farce, which describes the inanity of evil, which laments the poverty of poetry just as it demonstrates its power, and which encompasses history, politics, family and love is no small achievement.'
Times Literary Supplement

£6.99   1 85702 568 7

GABRIEL'S LAMENT
Paul Bailey

Shortlisted for the 1986 Booker Prize

Gabriel Harvey was a happy enough child. He would often sit in the gaslit kitchen of his modest terraced house listening to his father's memories of a deprived childhood. But when his father comes into some money, things take a turn for the worse. His beloved mother disappears and all Gabriel can do is dismiss his father's explanations, and find his own way of bringing his mother close to him.

£6.99   1 85702 588 1

All Fourth Estate books are available from your local bookshop, or can be ordered direct (FREE UK p&p) from:

Fourth Estate, Book Service By Post, PO Box 29, Douglas, I-O-M, IM99 1BQ

Credit cards accepted.

Tel: 01624 836000   Fax: 01624 670923

Or visit the Fourth Estate website at: www.4thestate.co.uk

*Prices are correct at time of going to press, but may be subject to change. Please state when ordering if you do **not** wish to receive further information about Fourth Estate titles.*

9 780007 292776